THE TURKEY FEATHER TRIO

P. RAY LEWIS

ISBN: 978-1-7372953-2-7

DEDICATION

This book is dedicated to my first wife, Leisha Lei Bolen-Lewis, who passed away in June, 2020. She was an avid reader and my greatest champion of the pieces I wrote. I valued her opinion above all others and the memories of that magical time and place that we shared will always be dear to my heart.

CONTENTS

ACKNOWLEDGMENTS

For this my first book, I would like to acknowledge my mentor, Mr. Danny Kuhn, who has patiently helped guide me, collaborated with me, and given me the privilege of sharing his own works with me before they were published. He accepted me on an intellectual level way back when, despite my not taking either of his classes in high school. I have always regretted not doing so. Danny has nudged me along and kept me going on this thing we call writing. I would also like to acknowledge Senator John D. "Jay" Rockefeller IV for his encouragement by telling me I was a good writer on more than one occasion. My gratitude to both of you.

CHAPTER ONE

It seemed like what he felt he wanted to do at the time which is why Mister Bill Handley was there in the first place. "There", mind you, was the Turkey Feather Rehabilitation and Assisted Care Life Center. Bill always thought the name sounded like one of the Pentecostal churches that had imprinted itself on his backside as a child.

Turkey Feather housed indigent seniors tiptoeing on the outer edge of existence. It was a southern-style mansion that sat high atop a steep hill just outside the city limits of Nickleville. The house seemed to peer down as if it was guarding against any unwanted guests. It looked as if it was maybe even hiding secrets of some kind beneath its rolling lawn. Strange clumps of various types of shrubbery were planted in disarray all over the estate. When the blades of grass on the slopes grew taller in the summer, they swayed in the wind and looked like an invisible herd of some wild animal was running through the fields.

Even the air around Turkey Feather carried the scent of mold mixed with rotting leaves. Antiquated, red bricks were softly crumbling at their edges and enormous lengths of ivy climbed along the corners of most of the buildings. The panes of glass were so old they ran in their frames exposing their age. Patches of pale-green moss and twigs were strewn over the clay tile roof and the gutters were rusted and clogged with leaves and acorns. Most of the pathways on the grounds were trampled down to packed dirt paths by the nomadic elders who had nothing more to do than wander the property.

The driveway at Turkey Feather was kind of unique. It snaked its way up the hill in two large arcs ending at the front of a nearly dilapidated mobile home. At the top, a few pin oaks and black walnuts towered over the patio outside the dining room window. The trees gave shade and at least one or two of the residents were always lounging beneath their sprawling boughs on most any day throughout the summer. They watched the ghosts on the front lawn dance and play. Most of the time, they'd simply lie there for hours contemplating God knows what and move only if the shade did or if someone mentioned a meal was being served or that tobacco was being rationed out. The entire place seemed run down and somewhat gloomy, but, for Bill, Turkey Feather held a charm unlike anything he had ever experienced.

While Nickleville wasn't even a dot on the map, it possessed a world-renowned reputation for whitewater rafting. Despite its sleepy demeanor, the rafting companies in Nickleville had a combined reputation for partying and raucous tourist groups. Occasionally, one of the rafters literally got carried away and was swept through the rapids ripping along the gorge below the town. Sadly, though, any idea of thrill-seeking or rafting trips was long gone from the minds of the folks at Turkey Feather. Theirs was mostly an existence of longing; longing for the past or longing for the end but a lonely and nagging longing nonetheless that drained their souls.

When Bill first arrived at Turkey Feather, the rehabilitation part was a joke. Not that anyone was anxious to be rehabilitated to begin with. The residents watched a lot of television and stood around outside smoking their cheap cigarettes every couple of hours. During Christmas, there were bingo games and the ladies' auxiliary from the local church came by once a month to "hold services". To be fair, it was hard to find interesting activities for a group of feeble seniors and, to say the least, no one really had much ambition at Turkey Feather. After all, it was the end of the line before the end of the line and that's not much of an incentive.

People usually came to Turkey Feather pretty much the same way. They stood in the parking lot looking the place over like they were inspecting it for something, but they just weren't quite sure what it was they were looking for. Their "beloved one" who had so graciously brought them there, would silently emerge from the car, scribble their signature on the piles of paperwork, and unpack the belongings for them all in the same breath. Each story was about the same. Their family wasn't able to care for them anymore. It was either financial burdens, or healthcare costs, or they were just not doing as well as they should be and they "feared for their safety".

A quick handshake, or a hug, and a wave good-bye and the decisions to be made were final. Most of their worldly belongings, and almost all of their dignity were now fleeting memories. They were on their own again just like the first time they had left home for good. People usually stayed at

Turkey Feather for a few years, or, until they were completely worn out. By then, it was time for a full-scale nursing home, or the "Glue Factory" as they resentfully referred to it.

Surprisingly, though, everyday life at Turkey Feather was pleasant. The staff tried to make things as comfortable and enjoyable as possible given the circumstances and the residents all got what they needed. They ate hot meals three times a day along with a couple of snacks to break up the monotony. The nurse aides helped with hygiene and filled out a lot of paperwork, and the living Quartets were straightened at least every other day.

Turkey Feather employed a one-man maintenance crew as well. He was a middle-aged fellow named Frank Gillespie. Frank always took too many long breaks out in the tool shed but he kept the place well-groomed and well-lit. He did his best to keep it all in working order, but it was old like the people who lived there, and he battled to stay ahead of the deterioration. A constantly leaking roof kept everyone busy catching water in buckets or Frank on a ladder patching spots in the ceiling.

The staff catered to the residents and teased with them a lot to help lift their spirits. Frank had a few "trusties" he let help him with his duties from time to time, too. Fortunately, no matter how stressful the conditions were, people at Turkey Feather usually grew to become more like a big family. There were occasional grumblings over the menu and bathing had to be scheduled due to the poor hot water circulation, and there was also a dullness that hung in the air most days. All in all, though, everyone tolerated one another's quirks and tried to get by without incident.

Bill had majored in Gerontology and Social Work at a private college in west Texas that was trying to restructure its image and bring in new programs. They offered a discounted rate to anyone who agreed to be a test subject for the new degree in aging issues.

"What the heck…," Bill thought. "I'll be old, too, some day."

Of course, no one ever bothered to tell Bill that a Social Work salary would be so pathetic. He learned that all on his own while he struggled to pay off mountains of student loan debt.

Bill found out about Turkey Feather through a friend named Larry Black. Larry had spent a year in the Nickleville area when he was younger. He remembered Bill's enthusiasm about the seasons and their changing weather. Bill got Larry's call during a break at the children's shelter where he was completing his post-graduate internship.

3

Larry told him about the job and how the last guy had left because of personal reasons which, knowing Larry as well as he did, sounded to Bill an awful lot like some scandal had been attached. Larry assured Bill he would love the place. While he was skeptical at first, after Bill's arrival (and much to his surprise), he decided Larry had been right. He was pretty sure it was the only time he ever remembered Larry being right about anything.

After talking to Larry, Bill called the owner of Turkey Feather, Mr. Rounder, who was apparently desperate because he did the phone interview and hired him all in the same conversation. He only paused once to come up for air. Still hesitant, he thought it over for a few more days before accepting. Over the next ten days, he packed everything he could cram into his prized forest-green convertible 1966 Mustang and headed out.

Bill loved that car, old as it was. He had bought it just after starting college from an older fellow who had plans of restoring it. Unfortunately, the man couldn't quite get his heart to cooperate with the plan. So, after a couple of hours of talking to him about his "condition", Bill got a pretty good deal on the clunker. Maybe learning how to deal with codgers hadn't been such a waste after all.

When Bill finally arrived at Turkey Feather, it was past the first part of autumn and a lot of the trees Larry had mentioned were changing. The colors dotted the countryside as he drove along the highway and the air had a crispness to it that brought a smile to his face. Bill rode up the winding driveway and parked underneath one of the pin oaks being careful to avoid getting too close for fear the acorns might fall into the seats and further dull their faded covers.

Bill climbed out of the car and walked over to what he thought was the front door. When he knocked, a short brunette about his age looked at him and pointed to the side. He walked around and waited for her there.

When she let him in, she smiled up at him.

"You must be the new boss we've been waitin' on. Come on in. My name's Sammie. Sammie Miller."

He followed her inside.

"Thanks, I'm Bill Handley,"

"Nice to meet you. Come on in."

"Nice to meet you, Sammie. Thank you."

When they got to the entrance of the kitchen, Sammie introduced him to the cook. Hilda Ferrell was a big woman with a wide face. She was part Cherokee Indian and part Irish. Hilda usually dressed in sweatpants and a t-shirt and today had a butcher's apron hanging from around her neck. She stuck her hand out with a goofy but kind grin.

"Howdy, there – nice to meet ya!"

"Nice to meet you," he replied as Sammie led him through the kitchen and out behind the building.

"Don't talk too much to Hilda. She's a troublemaker," Sammie whispered.

Bill nodded his head and gave her the thumbs up gesture, promising he would be careful. Sammie took him all around the grounds pointing out everything that was wrong with the place. She told him about some of the two dozen residents who lived there and how their personalities all managed to intermesh with one another even though they were all still quite different. During their walk, the residents didn't seem to pay too much attention to them just nodding and half smiling as they passed.

After what seemed to be at least a couple of hours, Sammie and Bill went back into the main building where she led him down the first-floor corridor. They glanced into the residents' rooms and then went upstairs to the make-shift dormitory in the loft. The place didn't look too bad at first glance, but it surely needed regular maintenance with that many elderly people housed in one area.

Bill looked around a little between Sammie's dialogue. In front of the kitchen was a small sitting room with an ancient black and white television and a couple of love seats shoved up against the walls. A smaller door under the stairwell to the loft hid the steps to the laundry room in the basement. Past the sitting room and off to its left was a large, open dining room where most of the activity at Turkey Feather took place. There was a nice church-style upright piano sitting in the foyer just outside the dining room. The acoustics were surprisingly good in the old haunt which allowed the piano to easily be heard throughout the building.

Sammie took Bill to the tin shack outside the main building. To his dismay, it was the "Administrative Office," only an outbuilding with a flimsy aluminum door, but the window in the back looked over the grounds of Turkey Feather several miles down the gorge. Bill was also pleasantly surprised at how much beauty squeezed into that tiny, little window frame.

5

Along one wall was an old sofa where several discarded magazines and newspapers were stacked. Most of the space along the rest of the walls was taken up by metal filing cabinets filled with records from years past. The desk was a metal beast that school principals typically have in their office. On one corner of the desk sat a phone and a fax machine, both of which looked to have been at least as old as Methuselah. Over in a corner behind the desk was a cardboard box full of what looked like games and prizes. The entire place reeked of mildew.

Bill sighed. It was a wreck by the best standards.

"Pretty bad, huh? Our last boss, Peyton Davies, didn't take very good care of the place so I guess you inherited his mess," Sammie grinned.

"I've seen worse, I guess, but it's been a while."

They both laughed, and Bill realized then that Sammie was on his side. It's a comforting thought when you're the new guy in town. It always helps boost your confidence to have someone rooting for you before the game even starts.

They talked for a while longer. Sammie told Bill of her impending divorce from a man her father had wanted her to marry when she was way too young. She had a six-year-old girl and two-year-old little boy who tied up most of her time, but she adored them both. Sammie was a nice girl and she cared about the residents of Turkey Feather immensely. She regretted dropping out of high school and wanted to get her GED someday. Maybe even go to college. From the conversation, he could tell Sammie had lived a rough life. She wanted more for herself and her children but didn't quite know which direction to take or how to go about making the necessary changes because no one ever showed her how. Bill decided he could help her best by encouraging an education. Costly as they may be, they still opened a lot of doors. Student loans, on the other hand, were another problem.

Sammie locked the office door and she and Bill talked more as they walked to the trailer at the end of the driveway. They waded through a litter of kittens that seemed to multiply before their very eyes. Sammie rang the doorbell. A stumpy, middle-aged woman greeted them. She cracked open the door and peered out suspiciously.

"Hi Lucy, this is Bill Handley. He's our new boss. Whadaya think?"

"I think he couldn't do any worse than that Peyton. He was a horse's puh-toot if you ask me."

6

Sammie and Bill both chuckled to themselves.

"I'm serious! He was dumb - and he was mean to them patients, too. He wouldn't give 'em their money like he was s'posed to and he drank up ever'thang this place took in. That's why we're in the shape we're in now cause of him!"

Another eye-opening revelation about Turkey Feather that Larry conveniently forgot to mention. It seemed from listening to Lucy and Sammie talk about Mr. Davies, things were a little tight in the finance area. Bill began wondering if he was in for more than he bargained for.

They bid Lucy farewell after some more small talk and headed back to the main building. It was time for the next shift to come in and Sammie to leave. Before she left, Sammie introduced Bill to Tina Dennison, a dark-haired, olive-skinned girl in her mid-thirties who cooked some when needed. Her main job was housekeeper, but Tina took care of the laundry and straightened the living Quartets on the side. Sometimes she helped Sammie with the hygiene needs when they worked together. Tina seemed quiet but had a friendly smile like Sammie's. That was one of the nicer things that struck Bill about Turkey Feather. Everyone smiled a lot and seemed genuinely nice. Bill took that as a good omen.

The evening shift never had more than two people working because all they had to do was warm up the dinner Hilda had cooked earlier in the day, hand out medication, finish the laundry, and ration cigarettes and tobacco. Lucy popped in and waved as she headed into the kitchen to put her things away. She always brought her diet food in a plastic container. Tina and Lucy got everything squared away about the time Bill decided to call it a day.

He said his farewells and climbed back into the Mustang. As he started down the drive, the air hit him again with a fresh crackle and he smiled even bigger than he had on the way in. Bill felt pretty good about things by now, so he decided to treat himself to a banana split.

At the Dairy Barn down the road, Bill stared into oblivion and thought about Turkey Feather. He thought about how fate had dealt such a strange and cruel hand to the people there. He thought about how they had all been brought together at a friendly prison of sorts. He wondered about their lives, their loves, and the dreams they once held. It made Bill sad to realize how things must have turned out so very differently than what they had expected.

Bill left to look for the house he had arranged to rent in Beech Knoll, the next town over from Nickleville. Larry helped him secure the place before he came in, but this was the first time he would see it. Bill relished playing the daredevil, sight-unseen renter, but was kind of worried about what Larry may have stuck him with. After a quick stop at the grocery store, he headed to his new digs.

The house was easy enough to find. Bill drove through the opening in the chain link fence and parked in back against the rear deck. Hesitantly, he leaned over onto the passenger's side seat and looked up at the outside of the house. Gray siding and navy-blue shutters, new windows, a good roof – this could be promising. Bill got out and stood next to the car for a moment and surveyed things for a while. He was beginning to think he had been too hard on Larry in college because the place was a lot nicer than he had expected.

Bill walked up the steps and tried the key Larry had mailed him a few days earlier. As the lock turned, he breathed a sigh of relief. The door creaked as it opened. Bill peeked inside and what he saw was completely astounding. A neat kitchen, small, but replete with every appliance imaginable. There was a kitchenette in the corner and the curtains weren't too girly. He went through every room and found more and more treasures in each one. A cushy recliner, a sofa, and a newer model cable-ready television in the living room. The bedroom had a queen-sized bed and a pair of nightstands he could lay his books on. There was an enormous walk-in closet with plenty of shelf space in the master bedroom. The bathroom even had a spa tub and shower with a big towel cabinet filled with new linens. Even the toilet looked new.

Bill couldn't believe it. The place was perfect. Not too frilly but soft enough to relax even the most stressed-out Social Worker. Ol' Larry must have felt guilty about stiffing Bill on all those bar tabs in college because he really did a good job setting him up here. He made a mental note to give Larry a call and thank him when he got a chance.

After a day like this, all Bill wanted to do was crash on the recliner and turn on a quiz show for some brain-drain. He woke up four hours later just as the local news was ending. Bill made his way into the bathroom, took his contact lenses out, and crawled under the bed covers planning to reflect on the first day of his new job.

The next thing Bill remembered was being wakened by sunlight shining through the blinds. The alarm clock hadn't sounded yet. He laid there for a few more minutes and planned his day. His thoughts returned to the people at Turkey Feather, and he shook his head in disbelief at all of it.

Bill ran through his normal morning "man routine", slathered a gob of peanut butter on some toast and grabbed a small bottle of grape juice as he was heading out the door. He walked into Turkey Feather just as Sammie was cleaning up after breakfast.

"Mr. Rounder will be here a little later this morning. He called a few minutes ago," Sammie smiled.

"Thanks," Bill told her. He was grateful for the extra time that would give him a chance to straighten the office as best as he could. While he waited, he decided to let Mr. Rounder sit behind the desk out of courtesy. After all, he was the owner of Turkey Feather and that's how Bill was raised. Respect your elders or anyone else who was in charge for that matter.

When Mr. Rounder arrived, he stepped quietly into the office almost catching Bill off guard while he was looking out his favorite little window.

"Hi there," he said dryly looking past Bill as if he wasn't there.

Bill recognized his voice from the phone interview.

"Hello. Nice to finally see you face-to-face, Mr. Rounder."

"Yeah, kid. Same here. Name's John by the way. Look - I'm a busy man. I'm sure you can tell that from our phone conversation. I know this place is a wreck and it's run down so I don't expect a lot from you. Just take care of things and make sure no one gets hurt and sues me. I'll be happy with that. Everything you need to know you can find out from the girls or Frank. Watch Hilda – she's a troublemaker. Everybody else is okay. If something happens like the roof falls in or you spring a big leak, let me know. I don't want to have to spend too much in repairs so try to have Frank do as much as possible. Other than that, I can't offer a lot more so you're pretty much on your own here. Call me if you need me."

"I'll do that. Thanks a lot for coming by."

"Take care, kid."

Mr. Rounder walked out of the office without so much as shaking Bill's hand. He slid into a silver Cadillac and roared out of sight. Bill would never see him again the rest of his time at Turkey Feather.

Things were pretty clear. Not only had the residents' families abandoned them, but Turkey Feather itself had been abandoned. The only thing positive each had going for them was the staff and now Bill. Turkey

Feather was the place no one wanted to acknowledge existed because it scared them to think they could end up there, too. The whole situation made Bill instantly feel sorry for the residents. He decided then and there to make things better one way or another. Bill knew he had a hard row to hoe, but he was determined to do right by Turkey Feather, so he started to formulate his plan.

"How did the meeting with Mr. Rounder go?" Sammie asked when Bill came back into the dining area.

"Pretty good, I guess. He doesn't have much to say and he seems all business to me."

"He is. You'll probably never see him again. You're officially the boss now." Sammie winked at him as she walked into the next room with a laundry basket under her arm.

About that time Bill heard a voice call from the hallway.

"Hey, I bet you don't know who hit the most home runs in 1957, do ya?"

It kind of took Bill by surprise because he assumed no one at Turkey Feather would have an interest in baseball. The voice was from none other than that of Turkey Feather's one-man quiz show and sports aficionado, Tilson Raft – Tilly for short.

Bill gave Tilly his best guess for an answer.

"Is wasn't Hank Aaron, was it?"

Tilly looked at him with his mouth half open like Bill was a full-blown trivia deity.

"Aaat's riiighttt! Boy, yer a smart man! I bet you know a lot of stuff. You're good. Hammerin' Hank Aaron! Aaat's riiighttt!" he drawled.

Sammie stepped in before Tilly could get any further.

"Tilly, are you botherin' the new boss?"

"No, I am not. I'm just talkin'. He knows a lot about sports – see, ask him."

"Here's a cigarette, Tilly, why don't you go outside and smoke for a while."

At the mention of the word "cigarette", a flash mob of elderly nicotine addicts rushed the hallway closet nearly knocking Bill and Sammie down. Bill thought he might be trampled at one point but managed to move out of the way until the tobacco turbulence was over. He watched in silent shock as each of the tobacco lovers indulged in their favorite past-time. Bill decided they absolutely had to find better hobbies for these people. This was ridiculous.

Sammie told Bill all about Tilly. Tilly had battled schizophrenia most of his life. He drifted around and worked a lot of labor-type jobs in sawmills and lumber yards but never really made much of a life for himself. In all actuality, he never really had a chance to make a life for himself. The schizophrenia had pressed down on him his entire adult life. Tilly talked about being abused and electrocuted at one of the state hospitals. Bill suspected he meant that he had undergone shock treatments. He was sure that sort of thing was something you just couldn't put behind you when you didn't understand what was going on to begin with.

Tilly had a flair for trivia, though, especially sports trivia, and he was always trying to get people to play his guessing games with him. Tilly's focus on sports made Bill imagine he had fantasized about playing professional sports but could never pull things together to remotely do anything of the sort.

Bill talked to Tilly a while longer until he couldn't think of anything else to be grilled on and any more trivia to be questioned about. After leaving Tilley, he walked around on his own asking some of the other residents how they were doing and how they felt. They all had a story to tell about what the doctor had told them last and how they hated taking all the medication they were on and how they didn't put much stock into what doctors said anyway. Bill nodded a lot and just listened. That small gesture alone seemed to do wonders for everyone he spoke with. Bill figured correctly that it had been a long time since the people at Turkey Feather had someone to really listen to what they had to say. He could tell it made them feel good to have someone to "talk" to even if they were only listening.

During his conversations, Bill noticed one group of residents that didn't interact much at all with the others. There were four of them. Each one silver-haired and so distinguished in appearance they really didn't look like they belonged at Turkey Feather. This was a peculiar bunch of gentlemen indeed. They all carried a slight stoop to their shoulders and their gait was deliberate. The way they dressed reminded Bill of a gang of college frat boys waiting for a chance to play practical jokes. The quartet was certainly a welcome change of scenery. Bill introduced himself.

"Hi there – name's Bill Handley. I guess you could say I'll be runnin' things around here for a while."

With a glint in his eye, the tallest gentleman held out his hand and gave him a toothy grin.

"We heard. Welcome aboard, Sport."

The one who looked like a Native American chimed in.

"Yeah – welcome to the Glue Factory."

Another one spoke up.

"Glue Factory? This ain't the Glue Factory! This here is the Dog Pound! This is where they leave all us old hounds BEFORE they take us off to the Glue Factory, unless they put us to sleep first."

He smiled at Bill and then poked his friend in the ribs. The Indian let out a sort of half-laugh and half-wheeze and then stood up straight to make his announcement.

"You, sir, have arrived at the Turkey Feather Rehabilitation and Assisted Care Life Center. Welcome to our most humble abode."

He saluted and then bowed at the waist like an English butler. Bill couldn't help but laugh at their camaraderie. These guys were a hoot. He also couldn't help but ask about their choice of attire.

The tall one spoke again and informed him of their status.

"Well, I guess you could say we're waitin' on a ride of sorts. We don't have any place to go, and we haven't decided when we're goin' but we like to be ready just in case. Who knows? We might end up goin' on an adventure with Tom Sawyer and Huck Finn."

The Indian looking man spoke again.

"Awww… don't pay no 'tention to him. He likes to talk in circles sometimes and ya cain't hardly figure out what he's talkin' about. He's like the rest of us!"

They all laughed together at that declaration. They motioned for Bill to sit down with them. As he did, the gentlemen began to tell their stories one by one. The tall gentleman was Lester McManamay. Lester was a retired schoolteacher whose wife had died years ago. Lester and she never raised a family. Turkey Feather was all he had. His brothers and sisters had died and none of his nieces ever wrote or visited. This was his only family. Lester was acutely aware of his situation which is why he came up with the idea for him and his pals to move in together. He was the leader of the pack and the orneriest one of them all. Lester was also the slightest bit feeble and used a cane – for support purposes only, he assured everyone. Funny and good-natured, there was no getting Lester down regardless of how tough things got. Lester would later prove to be a special inspiration to Bill.

The next man was Raymond Hardy. He swore he was a distant cousin of the famous Oliver Hardy and that Oliver had been very fond of him when he was a small boy. Oliver had even taken him to some of the film sets he worked on to meet the all the Hollywood Land stars. The famous Hardy had supposedly created a trust fund to pay for Raymond's private education. Raymond went on to tell Bill that his mother died when he was ten and his father married a much younger woman who only cared about spending money. His new stepmother found out about the trust and insisted the money be used to help fund a lavish lifestyle for her and Raymond's father. Raymond left home when he was fifteen and didn't keep in touch with his father much after that. He told Bill how his father had apologized right before he died about the way he treated Raymond and that he had set aside some of the money in the trust for Raymond to use later in life. Unfortunately, the paperwork had gotten lost down through the years and the bank where his father had opened the account had been closed for a long time. With the wit and humor Raymond possessed, Bill could almost believe the story as ridiculous as it sounded. He suspected it was really a big lie Raymond had created in his mind to ease the pain he felt over being broke and alone.

Raymond had never been married and didn't have a family that anyone knew of so there was no way to check his story out. He was always carrying on with some nonsense, so his credibility was questionable. Raymond was a great guy, though, and you could always count on him to be straight with you when things were serious. Bill liked Raymond but they all had to watch out for whoopee cushions and fake doggy-doo that he occasionally and strategically placed throughout Turkey Feather. Racin' Ray is what they called him because of the way he made motor sounds with his mouth and ran away from the scene of his latest prank.

Fred Whiteowl was the Native American. Fred had been raised on a reservation in Oklahoma and had found his way to Nickleville by way of the coal mines. He married his high-school sweetheart, Rose, and raised eight children with her. She had left Fred for reasons no one could ever figure out.

Naturally, Fred was one of Hilda's favorites and she snuck him biscuits when no one else was around. It was a nice thing to do for the old man, but Fred was diabetic and that made the extra biscuits a huge problem. Hilda knew better and had been warned about it by the nurse, but she ignored the warnings until she had to be threatened by management which was Bill's job now.

Fred was the feeblest of the four and drifted off into long, deep stares from time to time. Sammie told Bill that Fred was sad a lot and thought about his family when he stared into the distance like that. She only hoped it wasn't the beginning of Alzheimer's.

Bill would soon find out that Alzheimer's was like God...it always had a way of touching people in mysterious ways. Besides cancer, Alzheimer's was just about the cruelest thing Bill had ever seen. Its victims were robbed of the very essence of their lives and the sad part was that it struck so quietly, they never had a chance to defend themselves. They just slipped away from everything they knew without knowing anything had ever happened.

Fred had a child drown when the boy was sixteen and he never seemed to get over it. His second-youngest daughter, Kaye, was the only one that ever really came to visit him. She had a family of her own to take care of and didn't get a chance to come by as often as she liked. Fred could turn on a guilt trip, though, and Kaye lived hard when he felt neglected. He had an emotional hold over Kaye that made her feel she had to please him no matter what. Fred's other children called from time to time but never visited with him like they could have. Bill guessed that Fred's daydreams were sometimes just trips down memory lane.

The last member of the "Quartet" as Bill came to call them most of the time was Mavis G. Polnicheck. Mavis was a character unlike the rest of the bunch simply because of the life he had lived. He had been a regular rolling stone and a real bravado in his day. Mavis had been married at least four times and had about a dozen kids the best he could remember. Mavis said he had been a spy for the Air Force and told so many stories of fantastic proportion that no one believed a word he said. He loved life and was one of the liveliest old men Bill had ever seen. Mavis chased Sammie and Tina, too, every chance he got and gave them more than a few bruises from pinching them on the rear end. Bill had to warn Mavis about that behavior so many times that it was almost like he did it just so Bill would take him to the side and scold him while his companions watched and giggled from the sidelines. Mavis was a daredevil, the class clown, and a dirty old man all rolled into one.

The Quartet never made too much trouble for anyone but

14

themselves and aside from giving Hilda a well-deserved migraine from time to time, they were harmless. They really livened things up and broke the monotony of an otherwise mundane existence. Bill enjoyed every minute with them, though, and loved hearing their stories – especially the ones Mavis told. Those yarns were so hilarious they could make Bill laugh until he cried. He often wondered if there was something Mavis was hiding. Each story he told was so far-fetched the only thing funnier would have been if they were true. Bill noticed, too, that a lot of Mavis' stories seemed to have a hollow tone to them that quietly shined through. That hollowness was probably due, in part, to the fact that Mavis appeared to have a lot of regret in his life from all the lost loves and from not knowing who or where his children might be.

Listening to himself after a while, it seemed like Bill literally tried to analyze everything that went on at Turkey Feather. He had a lot of time to watch people because everyone at Turkey Feather had a routine that didn't change much unless they became ill or misplaced their eyeglasses only to find them hours later perched on top of their head. Time had a way of playing tricks on people's minds at Turkey Feather. Time just seemed to go too fast or too slow, but Bill could never seem to figure out which until it had already happened. Time is funny that way. You never seem to have enough of it until you retire and then you rush to keep yourself busy. That way you won't have too much time on your hands. Bill guessed it all boiled down, really, to folks just figuring out they're scared to death of getting old. They try to avoid becoming too big of a burden to anyone including themselves.

That's the way life went at the Turkey Feather Nursing and Rehabilitative Assisted Care Life Center. People wanted to be left alone because they had already been left alone and had forgotten how to respond to too much of anything else. Everyone just slid by and tried to remember how to be happy most of the time.

For the most part, grumblings were few and far between and life at Turkey Feather, for all intents and purposes, was good for the residents. Nobody wanted to make waves and most everyone accepted their lot in life knowing there was little they could do about it. No one wanted to make waves, except, of course, the Quartet and Hilda. Sometimes, after a hard day, that name alone sent shivers down Bill's spine.

Bill had been told by several folks that Hilda had a mean streak in her a mile wide that came out during some inopportune times. It usually happened when one of her favorite helpers hounded her for "treats" and she was running behind schedule. She would playfully smack their cheeks turning them red and then scold them like a child for aggravating her so much.

Most of the time her actions were harmless, but a few times, she got a little too rough. Sammie and Tina would tell Bill about it. Hilda never let him see things like that so he had to make sure not to play into the politics of possible jealousy among the girls when accusations were made. Bill tried to be fair and objective, but abuse was something he would have never tolerated, even if it had only been something playful or harmless.

Bill quickly grew to love Turkey Feather and the people it sheltered more and more. The residents were all like his own group of children, even though most of them were old enough to call him their grandson. Like the old saying goes, they were one big, happy family and to his relief, the first few weeks went by without incident. Bill reviewed files to get a better insight into what he had on his plate and the residents followed their own routines like always. Bill would never forget what happened next, though.

Just as he arrived one morning, he heard a blood-curdling scream that almost made him lose control of his bladder. He dropped his briefcase in the parking lot and ran into the main building.

"GGGAAAWWDDDAMMIT!!!   GGGAAAWWWDDDAMM NASTIES!!! YOU SONSABITCHES!!! LEA' US 'LONE!!!'" was repeated at least a dozen times at decibels nearing that of a jet airplane.

Sammie and Tina were wrestling a tiny hag of what Bill thought was a woman up out of the floor. They were trying to shove her through the doorway to the lower bedroom.

Sammie yelled at Bill.

"Bill! When we get her through the door, slam it shut and lean into it or she'll escape!"

She thrust her weight into the shriveled little troll again. Bill became immediately concerned.

Escape? What in the world was going on? At that moment, he was too startled to ask so he simply did as he was told.

Tina swiped her foot behind the hobgoblin and Sammie hooked her under the arms as they all three burst their way onto the edge of the closest bed.

Bill stood with a deer-in-the-headlights look until Sammie yelled again.

16

"Shut it! Shut it! Close the door before she gets out!" This had to be an animal of some kind!

Bill slammed the door tight and leaned into it as best he could all the while trying to keep from breaking out into a cold sweat.

Hilda popped her head around from behind the kitchen entryway.

"Did they get 'er? Man! She was wound up tight this mornin'! Good thing they got her back in that bedroom or she would have been runnin' all through the house nekkid as a Jaybird!"

She had another one of those goofy grins on her face that always made her look guilty of something or just plain stupid.

"WHAT IN THE HELL was THAT?" Bill asked as he stood there with his mouth gaping open.

"That was Claudia. She's demon possessed."

Even though the term 'demon possessed' wasn't quite the clinical terminology to be used, Bill had to agree with Hilda's diagnosis. He was still a little dazed when he replied.

"What's a Claudia?"

Hilda let out one of her bellowing laughs and slapped the countertop.

"They didn't tell you about Claudia? That woman's a wild cat. She don't weigh but about eighty-five pounds and could prob'ly throw me and you both around. Claudia's sister is a friend of Mr. Rounder's family and he promised we would take care of her until somethin' happened to her or we couldn't keep her anymore. This mornin' was mild compared to what I've seen her do before. I don't fool with her anymore 'cause she bit me one time."

"Great," Bill thought. "We've got a demented female pro wrestler on our hands."

About that time, Tina knocked on the other side of the door. In all the excitement, Bill forgot that he was holding her and Sammie in with the spawn of anti-Christ.

"You can let us out now! It's all right," she assured him.

He hesitated as he opened the door and looked in with one eye.

"Surprise! What did you think of Claudia?" Tina asked as she smiled a lot like Hilda had earlier.

"Well, she's certainly a spirited little thing!"

Bill's quick wit never ceased to amaze even himself.

"Wait until you've been kicked in the shin by that little thing," Sammie warned as she came up the ramp leading out of the room.

"That woman gets stronger all the time. Next time we're gonna wait for you to come in before we give her a bath. That way we can initiate ya."

"Uh... sounds like too much fun for me."

"You can wrestle her down while we clean her up."

"Yeah," Tina chimed in, "three men in a tub!"

She gave Bill a sly wink.

"What are we doing with a resident that hard to handle?" Bill asked, glancing from Hilda to Tina and then to Sammie.

"I's tellin' him about her sister and Mr. Rounder bein' friends with her," Hilda beamed.

"Yeah, I think they went to school together or somethin' like that, but I always thought there was more to it than that. Mr. Davies always handled Claudia's stuff and none of us ever saw any of her paperwork or anything," Sammie said.

She narrowed her eyes and looked at Bill with an inquisitive expression on her face.

Interesting... Ol' Man Beelzebub had probably forgot to sign her in when he dropped her off.

By now, Bill was starting to recover from his traumatic experience. It was time for him to make his first major decision.

"I think we need to find out more information on Miss Claudia. If she's that hard to care for, we're going to have to start handling her another way. She's going to hurt someone or get hurt herself if she keeps going off the deep end like that."

Everyone shook their head in agreement. Bill had seen a lot of adolescent teen-agers damage all sorts of property at the shelter, but it was unheard of for someone as old and seemingly fragile as Claudia to behave with what appeared to be superhuman gorilla strength. Then again, there was Hilda's demon factor to consider.

While Hilda went about her daily kitchen schedule, Sammie and Tina talked with Bill for a little while about all the antics Claudia had pulled during their tenure at Turkey Feather. Apparently, Claudia had attacked every single staff member that had ever set foot on the grounds of Turkey Feather at one point or another. She was known to sleepwalk at all times of the night and wander around the facility scaring unsuspecting personnel out of their wits. Claudia's favorite form of terrorism was streaking, and she gave the impression that she was quite uninhibited about her gnarled body. If anyone dared to cross her path, she would often shriek out a string of obscenities that would have made a seasoned ship captain blush like a choir boy.

Bill left Sammie and Tina to do their chores and walked out to the office. He started looking for Claudia's file and, to his surprise, it was missing completely. Now he was extra curious about Claudia's story. Bill rifled through some of the paperwork that hadn't been visited in a while when he heard someone whisper his name.

"Hey... Bill. Psst... Bill."

It was coming from the window. Bill raised up and looked into Tilley's big blue eyes staring right at him. After the morning he had just had, it startled him a little, but he kept his eyes fixed on Tilley in some hypnotic gaze.

"Would you run me down to the store and let me get a quart of chocolate milk? Please?"

Bill couldn't resist a request like that. Tilley sounded like a little kid.

"Do you have enough money, Tilley?"

"I got some money here in my pocket they give me from last time."

"You know you're supposed to put that back, Tilley, so nobody will take it from you."

"I know, Bill. Will you take me? Please?"

Bill decided he could use a shot of chocolate milk himself and a little trip to the local grocery store couldn't hurt either one of them.

19

"Okay, Tilley. Let's go."

"Thank you, old buddy. I like you."

"I like you, too, Tilley."

Bill and Tilley hopped into the Mustang and rolled on down the driveway. Tilley was a quiet passenger. He looked straight ahead out the windshield with a blank stare. Bill was afraid to think what was going on in that tortured mind of his.

Finally, Bill broke the silence.

"Where were you raised, Tilley?"

"Up the road there. Couple o' towns over. Whew, that's a long walk — 'bout fifty miles, I'd say."

"That far? That is a long way to walk. How did you get to Turkey Feather?"

"State brought me there. They kicked me out at the hospital. Said I's incorruptible. I was not. I wa'n't incorruptible. They just kicked me out."

"What do you mean by 'incorruptible', Tilley?"

"You know. They said I wouldn't do what I's told. They'd stick a finger in my face and say they's gonna kill me and my ancestors if I didn't do what they told me. They'll kill yours, too."

Bill had forgotten for a moment what Tilley's problem was. Schizophrenia had never been a specialty of his, but he was getting a first-class education. The sad part about all of Tilley's paranoia was that he believed every word he said. Bill supposed a lot of it had to do with the fact that most of what Tilley said probably was true. Tilley had lived one roller-coaster life judging from the bits and pieces Bill could string together.

"I don't think there's anything to worry about, Tilley. You're safe now."

Bill tried to reassure him as best he could but for some reason, he didn't think it helped much.

Tilley and Bill got to the store and just as Bill put the Mustang in park, Tilley jumped out of the car and walked into the store before Bill could catch up to him. Bill hurried into the store and walked down the main row peering quickly down each of the perpendicular aisles in a desperate attempt to find Tilley. Tilley was not the kind of fellow you just let run loose. Finally, Bill spotted him.

"Tilley! Where'd you go? I've been looking all over the store for you!"

Tilley looked at Bill with a half-hearted sneaky grin.

"Don't be mad, Bill. I's just lookin' for the chocolate milk."

"Well, now that you've found it, let's go. I don't appreciate you taking off like that from me. What if something happened?"

Bill had already started sounding like a mother hen. This man was old enough to be his own father and Bill was talking to him like he was a six-year-old.

Tilley paid for the milk and they both got back into the car. They didn't say much to each other until they parked at Turkey Feather.

"You ain't mad, are ya, Bill?"

"No, Tilley, I'm not mad. It just scared me a little when you took off so fast."

Tilley held up the three fingers on his right hand as a truce signal.

"I'm sorry, Bill. It won't happen again, I promise. Scout's Honor."

"It's okay, Tilley. Just remember that you promised not to do that again."

Tilley got out of the car and went inside with his quart of chocolate milk. By the time Bill walked in, half of the milk was gone. Bill stood in amazement at how fast Tilley could chug chocolate milk. Sammie scolded Tilley for drinking it so fast and Bill just shook his head as he walked down the hallway. He popped open the emergency exit at the end of the hallway and looked outside while he leaned against the door frame.

In the near distance, he saw the Quartet standing in a circle of sorts discussing what looked to be a very important matter. Bill decided to investigate but they saw him coming and scattered like schoolboys plotting some evil plan to vandalize the principal's house. To his surprise, Bill couldn't quite catch up to any of them before they found other residents to pair up with. Bill knew they were up to something, but he would have to wait for another chance to confirm his hunch.

It was close to the end of the day and Bill decided to go back to the office for a while and look at some more files. He still couldn't find anything on Claudia. Strange, very strange. There had to be something, somewhere, else how was her billing being processed? This was ridiculous. Payton Davies really must have been a jackass. Oh well. Not much Bill could do about it right now. He was exhausted and in need of some rest and relaxation. He walked out to the car and started it just as Sammie came running out.

"Hey, Bill! Please don't leave yet. Can I get a ride to the end of the road? My car is messed up and I need to meet a guy at the gas station out there so he can take me home."

"So, when did this 'boyfriend' come into the picture?" Bill asked grinning from ear to ear.

"Oh, he's not really a boyfriend. He's just one of my buddies I hang out with sometimes. How 'bout that ride?"

"Jump in."

Sammie got in, slammed the door, and they drove down the driveway. For some reason, Sammie didn't have much to say that day and Bill thought something might be bothering her. Better to let her bring it up than to pry he reminded himself.

They exchanged pleasantries at the gas station and Bill threw his hand up to the guy Sammie left with. He was a quiet sort with long hair. Looked like he probably even smoked a little weed maybe. To each his own, Bill thought, and he headed toward Beech Knoll.

When he got home, he crashed onto the sofa again. He began thinking about the day when he suddenly remembered the Quartet's strange actions. Those guys had to be up to something. But what? It couldn't be anything serious. Bill was sure it was just a practical joke at Hilda's expense which excited him. No need to worry, though, he'd find out sooner or later. They could never keep a secret too long.

CHAPTER TWO

The next morning at work, Bill tried to find the Quartet but none of the four were anywhere to be found. He asked Tina about them, and she informed him they had eaten breakfast and left.

"Left? Where did they go?"

"Didn't Sammie tell you about their trips? They go places sometimes, but they don't tell anybody where they're goin'."

"Isn't that kind of dangerous?" Bill asked as visions of an ambulance and bloody old men raced through his mind.

"Nah, they do it all the time."

Okay. Bill was super curious now. Those guys were doing something they probably shouldn't be. Mother hen or not, Bill was determined to find out. He ran all sorts of scenarios through his head placing them everywhere from getting beaten up by a gang of punk druggies to getting lost in another state. Bill was going to have to investigate this one.

He went out to the office and started rifling through some more of the files that Davies had left. Unfortunately, he still had no luck with the missing Claudia file. There had to be something that made her special. Why would anyone in their right mind take on that kind of responsibility? Too many mysteries and it was more than Bill could stand.

About that time Bill heard a knock on the office door. It was Wilma Pilkington. Wilma was one of those sweet little old ladies who had some trouble remembering. She suffered from a slight case of dementia but was never any trouble. She had a great smile to go with the stories she told about her younger days. It was funny to hear her talk about her experiences, especially when she would use the wrong word or mispronounce something which only added an innocent humor to her story.

"Hi there, big fella. Wha'd'ya know?"

"Not much, Wilma. You?"

"Oh - they got me cooped up in that place in there and I had to get out. I'm not one to stay cooped up like a chicken, ya know. I'm used to workin' for a livin'. I worked at the supermarket for forty years, but I'm retarded now. I got a pretty good pension from my husband, too. He was a railroader. He sure did railroad me a few times."

Bill stifled a laugh. Wilma was so funny.

"Wilma, what do you mean he railroaded you?"

"Oh, he promised me the whole gold mine but all I got was the shaft. Ever' time I turned around he was runnin' with some other woman. Finally, I got tarred of him and got me another man. I didn't marry that one, though. We just lived in sin till he went off to the war. Then I got another one while he was gone and had me a baby by him. My soldier boy come back and got mad and beat me up over it. He was a old bastard, you know what I mean?"

"Sounds like you had a pretty full love life, Wilma."

"Oh, I have. I have. I got me another man lined up if I can ever get him goin'."

"You be careful gettin' these fellas all riled up. You never know what might happen."

"Reckon' they'd blow a gasket?"

They both laughed. Bill promised her it was a possibility. Wilma left the office without saying anything more which was an odd habit of hers. As soon as she had said her piece, she just clammed up and walked away leaving you hanging. I think that was part of her charm, she always left you wanting more of the story.

As Wilma was leaving, Bill noticed some of the papers on the other side of the office that he had forgotten about. He walked over to the pile and picked up the top handful. It was then that he got his first clue as to what the

Quartet was up to. Bill could barely hear a couple of them through the office wall but not enough to be able to distinguish their voices.

Something was said about it being a mistake coming to Turkey Feather and what were they going to do now. It was time to crash the party.

Bill eased over to the door and undid the latch while holding it shut. He swung the door open just as Fred and Raymond were coming from around the back side of the office. They both looked like they had just been caught in the middle of robbing a bank. Their faces went white and their mouths hung open for a couple of seconds.

"What's up, boys?" Bill asked.

Fred stammered, "Uh…uh… nothin', Bill. Nothin'."

"Yeah, Bill, nothin' goin' on here. Just two old coots hangin' around enjoyin' the leaves," Raymond hesitated.

Bill knew something was completely wrong because there hadn't been any leaves on the trees for almost two weeks. He decided to push the envelope.

"Everything all right today?" he inquired with a cocked eyebrow.

"Oh, absolutely. Everything is fine, just fine." Fred assured him unconvincingly.

"Where are the other two?" Bill continued.

"They're here somewhere I s'ppose. I haven't seen 'em today."

Why were they lying? Tina had told him she saw the whole group eating breakfast this morning before they left. None of the four were ever very far from the others. It was almost like they all had a big secret to keep, and they wanted to keep an eye on each other. It wasn't a sinister feeling or anything ominous just interesting. Bill's curiosity was getting the best of him. He decided to let them off the hook and smiled as he left them to their own devices. When he got back inside, Sammie came rushing in.

"Bill, come quick. It's Lester. He's sick and I think we need to call an ambulance."

Bill jumped up and ran with Sammie to his room. Lester looked worse than anyone at Turkey Feather had ever seen him. He was bluish and sweating and looked like he couldn't gather his thoughts.

"Lester, are you all right?" Bill asked in his calm Social Work voice.

Lester looked around him like he was trying to figure out where he was.

"Hmm? What's goin' on here?"

Bill looked at Tina who had now joined him and Sammie.

"You'd better call the ambulance and tell them to get here right away."

Bill whispered to Sammie that he thought Lester may have suffered a slight stroke.

Tears welled up in Sammie's eyes and for a minute Bill thought he was going to do the same. They helped Lester back down on the bed and wiped his forehead. Tina brought an aspirin for him.

"Good idea," Bill told her.

They sat with Lester for what seemed like an eternity until the ambulance finally arrived. The paramedics did a preliminary check and moved him onto the gurney. Sammie got his chart from the office while the paramedics loaded Lester into the back of the ambulance. Before any of them thought to ask to go with him, the ambulance pulled out with a screaming siren and raced down the driveway.

Tina and Sammie looked at Bill. They all stood there for a second trying to figure out what to say. Rubbing the back of his neck, Bill took the lead.

"Let's hope everything is okay. Lester is a tough one so let's try to stay positive," trying to reassure them.

Sammie had tears rolling down her cheeks. Lester was about everyone's favorite, except for Hilda.

"I hate when one of 'em gets sick."

"Yeah, me too. It's like when one of my kids gets sick," Tina sniffled.

"Well, let's try to get through the day without upsetting everybody and if the residents have any questions, send them my way."
Bill went back out and sat down at his desk. Sure enough, in about thirty minutes, here came Tilley.

"Hey, Bill. What's wrong with Lester? He sick? I get like 'at sometimes. I get sick and my head feels all funny and I can't think straight. I do, boy, I sure do."

"Tilley! Just go back to the house and let things be right now! Go on! I mean it!" Bill fumed.

"Aww… I didn't do nothin'. Don't yell at me. I didn't do nothin' to ya. I's just tellin' ya. I'm gonna LEAVE here. 'at's what I'm gonna do. I'm gonna LEAVE here."

Bill immediately felt like he had kicked a puppy. The incident with Lester had them all upset, and Bill had taken it out on Tilley who was probably his biggest fan at Turkey Feather. Bill was in no shape to make an apology right now and he couldn't leave and force everyone to deal with Lester's probable stroke. Bill realized at that moment how fast you start to develop feelings for people you've only known for a few weeks. When people become such a big part of your everyday life, though, it happens before you even realize it.

Sitting in his office, Bill began to ponder his own life. What was he doing at Turkey Feather? Where would he go after this? Would that be him in Lester's place in forty years? There was always a lot to think about at Turkey Feather. but the future was especially difficult to consider when you had the opportunity to see its potential every day.

Bill knew he had to get his mind off Lester. so he went to find Sammie and Tina. They were sitting in the dining room smoking and staring out the window into nothingness.

"Hey. How's it goin'?" Bill asked.

Sammie put her thumb to her lip and stared down at the floor.

Tina looked up and forced a smile.

"Not bad. How 'bout you?"

"I'm okay. Just worried about Lester."

Sammie had a few tears still welling up.

"You think he'll be alright?"

"I hope so. Just try to be positive."

"I am but it's hard."

"Anybody seen Tilley?" Bill asked Tina.

"Not lately. He was in a bad mood earlier, though."

"Probably my fault. I was a little rough on him when we were trying to get Lester squared away."

After telling Tina and Sammie that they could take it easy for the rest of the day, Bill went looking for Tilley. At that very moment, he saw Raymond standing about twenty yards away. He saw Bill coming and hung his head like a kid who had been caught with his hand in the cookie jar. What is up with these guys today, Bill thought.

"Hey, Raymond. Where ya been all mornin'?"

"Oh... I just been goin' here and there. No place special. Lester gonna be okay? I sure hate him gettin' sick."

"I don't know Raymond. I think he might have had a stroke, but I won't know for sure until the hospital calls us. I'll let ya know when they do, though."

"Thanks. I'd appreciate that, Bill. Me and Les are close. We've knowed each other for a long time and I'd hate to see anything happen to him. He's a sharp one, that Les."

"Yeah, you're right about that, Raymond. He's smart alright."

Raymond began to shift his weight from side to side and Bill could tell he was in no mood to be questioned about what he and the rest of the Quartet had been doing. He reached out and patted Raymond on the shoulder. Raymond looked into Bill's eyes and tried to smile as best he could. They walked away from one another both thinking the same thing.

Bill gave up on finding Tilley and headed into the office again. He was determined to find something on Claudia, and he was going to find it today. He rambled through papers and files. About the time when he thought he had looked the entire place over for at least the third time, Bill heard something slide down the wall behind one of the metal filing cabinets. He leaned the cabinet away from the wall and spotted an accordion folder wedged between it and the cabinet. He stood there for a few seconds hoping this was the treasure he had been searching for.

Bill gently reached forward careful to not move the folder any further out of reach. He finally reached it and flopped it onto his desk. Slowly, he opened it and removed the contents. The first page had 'Claudia R. Saltzmann' written across the heading like an important letterhead. This was it. Bill had finally found the elusive "Demoniac Dossier". Unfortunately, there were only a few intake papers and not even enough of them to make a full packet. Still nothing solid to go on. Bill's level of frustration was growing more tense. There was no way that Claudia could have just appeared at Turkey Feather one day out of the blue without so much as a birth certificate or passport or anything else to identify her, where she came from, or how she landed in Nickleville. Bill flung the file across the room and ran his fingers through his hair.

The phone rang.

Hopefully, it was the hospital with word on Lester.

"Hello."

"Mr. Handley?"

"Yes, this is he."

"This is Rural Regional Health Center calling about Mr. Lester McManamay. It looks like he's going to be fine. He's a little dehydrated and had a little attack of exhaustion. We're going to keep him overnight for observation and we'll send him back first thing in the morning."

"I see. Well, thank you so much for calling. We'll look for him tomorrow."

Lester was suffering from exhaustion and dehydration. What in the world had he been up to? Bill thought for a second and then...THE QUARTET! Bill had his business hat on now and was about to call some old codgers out on the carpet. This was going to stop before someone got hurt.

He marched over to the main building and popped into the kitchen, his nostrils flaring. Hilda looked at him questioningly.

"What's up, Chief?"

"Hilda — have you seen any of the Quartet?"

"Nope. Not much of any of 'em today now that you mention it."

"If you see ANY of them, send them my way IMMEDIATELY."

"Will do, Chief. Sounds serious."

"It is. The hospital just called, and Lester had an exhaustion attack and is dehydrated. NOBODY at Turkey Feather gets exhausted and dehydrated and I'm going to find out how it happened."

Sammie came from the dining room.

"Hey, Bill. Heard anything on Lester?"

"I just told Hilda the hospital called and said he was exhausted and dehydrated. Explain that one!"

"Wow. Strange. Wonder what he's been doing?"

"Beats me but I'm going to find whoever knows something about it."

Bill went through the rest of the building looking for clues or anyone who might have clues. Not one remaining member of the Quartet was to be found anywhere. Apparently, they had left knowing they were about to be found out. He walked the grounds, too, but found no sign of anyone. Bill promised himself he would wait all night if he had to.

When it was time to go home, Bill still hadn't seen or heard from any of the boys. Somehow, he got the hunch to go to the hospital to see if he could get anything out of Lester. Bill knew with him being alone, he would have a better chance of getting the secret out of him. He left Turkey Feather without telling anyone his plan so he wouldn't have to turn anyone down who wanted to tag along. His next stop was a beeline for Rural Regional Health Center and Lester McManamay's hospital room.

When Bill got to Rural Regional, he introduced himself as a friend of Lester's. The Charge Nurse pointed down the corridor to Lester's room. Bill walked cautiously that way making sure he remained incognito as he kept an eye out for any of the Quartet. He was sure he might find them with Lester. When he found Lester's room, he could hear whispered chatter inside. With an unscrupulous smile that would shame the Devil, he knew if he listened outside the door, he would find out more than enough information on what that bunch of old crows was up to. He propped himself beside the door facing and, sure enough, the rest of the Quartet members were at Lester's side. Interesting...very interesting. He was close to finding out what this cockamamie game was once and for all, but he wasn't about to burst in on them without knowing what it was all about first.

"I knew we shouldn't have come here, Lester."

"Nonsense. You know as well as I do, we're close and we're not giving up yet. Just be patient, Fred."

"Yeah, Fred. We waited this long we can wait a little while longer. Cain't we fellas?"

"Raymond, you son-of-a-bitch. If we don't quit foolin' around like this, we're all gonna be found out and then the Feds are gonna bust in on us and everything will go to shit."

"Dammit, Fred. You're the single most paranoid ol' fool I ever met. That ain't gonna happen. Nobody cares enough about us to poke around in our business. Raymond – did you find that rope in case we need it?"

Rope? What did these guys need with rope? Bill couldn't believe what he was hearing. It sounded like his frail group of elder hostels was planning to rob a bank or something. It also sounded like they were nowhere near the guys everyone had all grown to know and love. With the mystery surrounding Claudia earlier and now this, Bill thought his brain would explode. He could barely hear them now, but he knew they were all riled up over something important. Some plan had gone awry. He inched closer to the door opening knowing he would have to be even more careful so they wouldn't catch him listening.

"That does it, you all. I'm outta here."

"Mavis! You leave now and I'll beat your ass to death with this bed pan."

"What? I ain't gonna stand here and listen to a bunch of ninnies cryin' around when we oughta be out there findin' that thing and gettin' it outta there."

Thing? What thing? Bill's heart was beating so fast he could feel the pulse in his ears. He thought he might have to flag one of the nurses down to check his blood pressure.

"Mav's right. Let's get back to business and sort this thing out when I get back to Turkey Feather."

"Okay, guys, but I ain't takin' no more chances like the other day."

"Don't worry your pretty head, Freddie, dear...nobody's gonna get

31

caught or hurt. We know when the time comes, all we gotta do is do it right and we're in the clear."

"That ain't gonna be happenin' unless'n you get your butt outta here, Les. You damned old coot."

"Thanks, Raymond. I'll be fine. Now you all get back and we'll talk more later."

With that, Bill spun on his heels and walked as briskly as possible to the front door just short of a full run. He hopped into the Mustang and got out of Dodge as fast as possible. Turkey Feather was too chancy right now with the boys coming back so he hurried home to gather his thoughts. This had been the single craziest day at Turkey Feather ever. First Claudia, then the Quartet. Bill pondered that life really isn't what it seems to be. Claudia's case had to be pitiful but what was up with the Quartet? Their situation was unexplainable and downright smelled of plain old no good at all.

That night, all Bill could do was roll back and forth in bed and kick the covers until his calves ached. The day's events played over and over in his mind for what seemed like hours. He was still thinking about Claudia and the boys when the sun poked through the blinds and spilled across his chest. Bill was going to have to find a way to thwart the boys or at least get an idea of what was going on. It wasn't going to be easy. These guys were on top of a game all their own for the moment.

From what Bill could gather by listening to the locals, the town of Nickelville was steeped in legends of defiant Confederate troops who used the cover of the rugged mountain paths to transport war supplies and spoils during the Civil War. More than one historian had written a book about the town and the ghost tours were popular every year, especially around Halloween. Nickelville was a simple and picturesque town but during whitewater season, strange tales of weird parties were rumored and occasional reports of a drowning or a missing person gave folks something more to talk about. The whole town really came alive in late summer and early fall when most of the local businesses were dependent on rafting season to carry them through the rest of the year.

People started finding out about Nickelville when the rafters and a few development companies started to stir the economy. It was a great place to live and raise a family and it seemed a shame that everything Turkey Feather stood for was just the opposite of the spirit of Nickelville.

The geography around the town was difficult to travel. Even the more seasoned hikers visiting the area had been known to lose their bearings amongst the trees and valleys. A person had to be in pretty good shape to walk the hills and hollers and climb around the cliffs of the gorge. Rattlesnakes were plentiful, too. Supposedly, the Division of Natural Resources had traded wild turkeys to a western state in exchange for rattlesnakes. At least that's what the old timers always said.

Turkey Feather itself was borne out of the Reconstruction period shortly after the Civil War. It was one of the first estates built in that part of the country and stuck out like a sore thumb in modern times. Its perch atop the hills in Nickelville gave it a watchtower effect like the mansion was locking or waiting for something, or someone, to return. Bill thought maybe it just had something to hide. It was hard to tell because there was a certain sadness that hung all around Turkey Feather. Maybe the place had arbitrarily accepted the personalities of its decrepit inhabitants or maybe it was just the melancholy tone of a bygone way of life. He could never put his finger on it. The place just drew one in like a call for help or a cry for someone to spend time with it. Of course, that's the way most of the residents felt, too.

Bill knew the Quartet's behavior was extremely odd. Their clandestine antics were out of character even for them. He was afraid they were really going to get hurt but he had to play along until he found out what it was all about. According to the girls, though, their frequent day trips were not out of the ordinary. Bill had imagined the Quartet to be volunteers at the hospital, reading to children at a library, or even going out bowling or chasing women. Who was he kidding, though? Bill knew it was something more. He kept thinking, please don't let it be illegal…please don't let it be illegal….

Lester arrived the next morning just as promised and seemed to be in great spirits. He joked with the girls and some of the other residents who asked him about seeing "…the Light at the end of the tunnel…". He and the boys (who had apparently also made it back all in one piece) were making their rounds as usual and things looked to be on their way to getting back to normal. Frank was raking leaves and working on some of the decorations for the upcoming holiday season when Bill stopped to see him. Bill and Frank never had much time to talk because Frank was always doing maintenance and Bill was always processing billing and filing papers.

"Hey, Frank. How's it goin'?"

"Oh, pretty good. You?"

"Okay, I guess. Lester had us all scared yesterday. The hospital said it was exhaustion and dehydration. I can't imagine that."

"Me either. Must be them hikes him and his buddies take."

"Hikes? What do you mean?"

"Ain't the girls mentioned it?"

"Well, they told me they go out sometimes but never where they go."

"Oh, they go to the parks and walk around and they go to the gorge and sometimes they just walk around here."

"What do they do on these hikes?"

"Beats me. It's like they're lookin' for somethin'."

"Looking for something?"

"Yeah. I've seen Lester with a big bunch of papers a few times and he was leadin' the others on what looked like a scavenger hunt to me."

Finally! My first real clue to what the Quartet was up to.

"Well, did you happen to ask them about it? I mean… about what they were doing?"

"Not really, I just nodded and asked what they were up to. They hollered back that it was nothin' so I nodded my head back to 'em."

"Do they go any place in particular that you know of?"

"Not really that I know of. I seen 'em take a cab outta here a few times lately, though. They catch it down at the end of the driveway down there. I ain't never seen much else."

"Thanks, Frank. You've been a big help."

"No problem. I'll tell ya if I see anything else."

"Right. Let me know if you see them getting in any more cabs, too."

This was all becoming really engrossing. Walking around Turkey Feather with a bunch of papers, going to the local parks, taxicabs to who knows where… this was going to be something worth watching. Bill began to wonder if he should bring Sammie and Tina in on it. Maybe just wait until he finds out more. Maybe he was making this out to be a bunch of paranoid over-analysis. He couldn't stop from obsessing about it now, though.

Bill hoped with Frank on guard that he would be able to catch a chance to follow the Quartet on one of their little jaunts, but he figured they were still too shook up from Lester's recent ailing to try anything daring at the moment. Bill watched them like a hawk and acted as if nothing was askew. Calm, cool, and collected he was. He didn't want to spook the boys at a crucial moment.

A couple of hours later, as Bill and Sammie were finishing lunch duty, Tina walked in to tell Bill there was a lady there to see him. She was the advocate from Adult Protective Services, Lorna Leonard. Lorna was standing in the middle of the sitting room when Bill greeted her.

"Hello, I'm Bill Handley."

"Mr. Handley, I'm Lorna Leonard."

"Nice to meet you, Ms. Leonard. What can I do for you?"

"It's about Tilson Raft. You know – Tilley?"

Oh God! Tilley! Bill had forgotten all about upsetting him. He broke out into a slight sweat. He had learned in college about the "Super Social Workers" known by "advocate". They had a penchant for giving other social workers the Third Degree and making their life sheer Hell whether innocently or not. That was just the nature of the job. Bill had dealt with child advocates before but never an adult advocate. One wrong answer or one bad report to the powers that be and the entire operation at Turkey Feather Rehabilitative Assisted Care Life Center could be suspended without so much as an appeal or a chance to appeal.

"Something wrong with Tilley?" Bill asked in the calmest voice he could muster.

"Not wrong, so to speak. I just wanted to make you aware that he has contacted our office and stated that he is taking himself off all his medications. That means he will not be taking his psychotropic meds. I've dealt with Tilley for several years, and this is a pattern he begins when he becomes upset. Has anything happened recently that you know of?"

Bill chose his words carefully. "Well, we did have a resident who was taken to the hospital yesterday. I believe that may have affected him."

"Could be. Usually, it's when someone yells at him or he gets into a verbal altercation of some kind. Anything like that?"

"Ms. Leonard, I'll be honest with you. I hope this won't have any influence on your report today. The patient I mentioned had all of us a little emotional and when Tilley asked me about him, I snapped at him a little. I didn't mean to upset him; it was just bad timing."

"I understand. Mr. Handley – Bill, if I may, I'm not here to make a report. I'm not one of "those" kinds of advocates. I know how it is here at Turkey Feather. I've been around the block a few times and I'm not fresh out of college with stars in my eyes thinking I can save the world. I just know how Tilley can get when he's not on his medication and I wanted to warn you. It can get nasty."

Bill let out a sigh of relief and Lorna chuckled. Thankfully, Lorna was a friend to Turkey Feather. Good to have someone of her standing willing to help.

"Sorry to make you nervous, Bill. That's just my title that does that. Don't worry. Tilley should go back on his medication in a couple of days or so. He's usually pretty good about his condition so just watch him and call me if you need any help."

"I appreciate your help, Lorna. Can I call you Lorna?"

"Sure. Just call me and let me know if anything happens. Mind if I talk to Tilley before I go?"

"Please. Be my guest. I'll get with him later today to talk about our miscommunication."

"Okay. Thanks, Bill. I'll let myself out when I leave."

A few minutes later, Bill saw Lorna driving away. Nice lady but he was glad that visit was over. It never seemed to fail that the uninvited guests at Turkey Feather were usually up to something that would create more work for you in the end. Lorna was the real deal, though, and didn't mind if the place wasn't spotless all the time or that some of the residents had a cold. Like she said, that was life at Turkey Feather and Lorna knew we were doing the best we could with what we had.

Bill waited until Hilda was setting up for dinner before he talked to Tilley. He found him sitting in a chair in the dining room rocking from side to side with his eyes closed. His hair was greasy, and he smelled sweaty.

"Tilley. How's it going?"

He opened his eyes slightly and gave Bill a cold look.

"Bill."

"Listen, Tilley. I wanted to apologize to you for fussing at you yesterday when you asked about Lester. That was no way for me to talk to you and I'm sorry."

"'at's alright. I ain't takin' no more medicine now, though. I ain't takin' no baths either."

"Lorna told me that you had called her to tell her you weren't going to take your medication. That's fine, Tilley, but if you get sick you might have to go to the hospital again."

"They ain't gonna keep me there, neither. I'll just go live in the streets like before. I ain't goin' to no hospital."

"I'm sorry Tilley. Really. I hope you understand that I was just worried about Lester."

"'at's alright. I's worried about 'im, too. Ain't nobody gonna talk to me like that. I ain't takin' my medicine no more."

Tilley closed his eyes and began rocking again. Bill stood there for a second trying to think of what to say to ease the situation but decided he should let it go for now.

"See ya, Tilley."

It was quitting time and it couldn't have been more opportune. When Bill climbed into the Mustang, it hit him to go to the local library and look up some history on Turkey Feather. It couldn't hurt to check on the place and see if there could be anything more on Frank's report of the need for a hunt. With all the Civil War history and a new idea that he might be looking for something important, Bill thought he could turn up something that might be helpful.

The library in Beech Knoll closed early in the fall so Bill hurried over there before he went home. He gathered up a few of the books on local history and checked them out. Bill was eager to scour their pages for clues. Back at the apartment, he flopped down at the kitchen table like he did when he was a kid in grade school. He pored over the musty tomes and looked at every page but there was nothing mentioned about Turkey Feather other than it was one of the first private residences to be built in the area. Seems it was situated close to some of the passage routes used during the Civil War, though. That could be something.

He looked at more of the information long into the night and began putting together more imaginative scenarios about what the boys could be looking for. It was treasure, he was sure. At least he hoped it was treasure. Everybody likes a good treasure hunt, and nobody is that secretive about looking for something if there's not treasure involved some way. Bill read a few more pages and then grabbed some shuteye. He dreamed all night of Civil War battles and ladies-in-waiting and the people of Turkey Feather. What a night.

The next morning, he picked up a documentary about Nickleville and, while sipping grape juice, ran across an intriguing story of a Confederate transport brigade that had been ordered to haul a small cache of gold through that part of the country. The brigade was supposedly ambushed, and the gold looted by a local militia. Rumor had it the ambush was bogus and the Captain of the brigade had conspired with his men to hide the gold in a cave nearby where they would recover it when their military service was over. That was the plan at least, until the Captain shot and killed his conspirators which gave credence to the ambush story. The cave was only known to a few folks who traveled the route on a regular basis. It was used as a shelter on winter journeys sometimes. The Captain was an extremely patient man able to wait a number of years before he went back to the scene of the crime. He knew it would look suspicious for him to come into too much money too soon after his military commission so when he returned to civilian life, he married a local girl and began to set up a series of small businesses to help elude suspicion. He made all the right moves and associated himself with all the right members of gentile society. The Captain then announced plans to build a grand estate. It was finally time for him to return to the cave. Apparently, though, the Captain's men had never trusted him and figured he had planned all along to double-cross them somehow. Upon his arrival at the cave, the gold was gone and the Captain was killed by an unknown fail-safe set by the men. Ironically, the Captain's wife continued with the construction of the estate and the businesses flourished making her one of the wealthiest women in the area.

Interesting, Bill thought. Maybe the Quartet was looking for the missing gold. Of course, they were in no condition to recover a wagonload of gold bricks but maybe there was something to the story that had put a gleam in their eyes. No one could say for sure. He just wanted them to quit running off trying to kill themselves doing whatever they were doing.

Bill was running a little late that morning. He had become way too enthralled in his history mystery and lost track of time. Sammie was working around the tables in the dining room and had a bigger-than-usual smile on her face for some reason.

"I hope that smile on your face means at least one of us got a good night's sleep."

"I guess so. I'm just happy today, that's all."

"Good for you. Kids okay this mornin'?"

"Yep - everything's fine and dandy."

"Good."

Sammie had styled her hair differently than usual, too. She was beaming and had a lightness to her step.

"Hair looks nice."

"Thanks. So. Whatcha' gonna teach me this mornin'?"

"Oh, I don't know. I have a few things on nutrition I want to go over with anyone who might be interested. I doubt I'll get much of a crowd, though. Senior nutrition isn't all that popular around here."

"Never know. Mind if I sit in? You might teach me something good that I don't know."

She half giggled when she looked at him and Bill thought she might actually be flirting a little. He took the bait and shot one back at her.

"You might could teach me a thing or two, girlie."

"Never know."

There was the giggle again. She was flirting.

Bill smiled and looked at her.

"That class might have to wait for later."

"Yeah. I don't want to overload your brain right now with too much information or anything. You might get excited."

"Hmmm…what possibilities."

Sammie grinned and walked out of the room. Just before she left sight, she turned her head and smiled directly at Bill, pausing while she looked. He felt a warming sensation in the pit of his stomach. What was he getting himself into? Sammie was nice, but, well... he'd just have to think about that later.

"GGGAAAWWDDDAMMIT!!! SONSABITCHES!!!"

"Oh, dear God," Bill muttered to himself.

Claudia was in rare form this morning and it was still early. Bill leaped into the hallway and almost crashed into Sammie and Tina who were rushing to Claudia's door. They made it into the room in record time but nothing else was coming out of the dragon's den. Claudia was asleep.

"Does she do that a lot?" Bill asked Hilda who was leaning on the shelf of the kitchen's half-door.

"Not s'much anymore. She used to do it a lot when she first come here. Now she just does it durin' the day when she sleeps real late."

Sounded like night tremors only a daytime version. Bill would have loved to have known what was going on in Claudia's head, but he suspected that no one would have ever been able to touch that realm. Bill was sure that Claudia had lived one difficult life to say the least and her memories and thoughts had been locked away from the rest of the world for a long time. She was like a lot of the residents of Turkey Feather in that sense. They spent most of their days in a quiet, self-imposed solitude and didn't let in much of anything that would disturb them. It was difficult to comprehend that silence. One would have thought that many people all living in the same place at the same time, would create more activity and disruption. Even though they all shared the same surroundings, they still managed to maintain their individuality through the boredom of their existence. Too many times at Turkey Feather boredom managed to overtake what little life was left and the people slipped away from knowing, or not knowing, anything at all.

With Claudia sleeping and everything, for the minute, looking like it was going to be a semi-normal day, Bill decided to try to talk to Tilley again. His nutrition speech must not have been at the top of anyone's agenda for the morning and he needed to get a handle on Tilley before he went too far with his medication strike.

Bill went up to his room to find him. What he saw was more than shocking. In the couple of days that Tilley had been off his medication, he had developed a crazed look in his eye and his hair stuck out like something you'd find in a werewolf movie. Tilley smelled of sweat and his stubble was patchy. His face oily. Bill couldn't believe the transition Tilley had made in such a short time. Tilley had always kept himself well-groomed and clean even though the medication he took made his fingernails grow long and brittle in a relatively short time. He was obsessed with washing his hands, another symptom of the schizophrenia. Tilley's shirt was matted to his chest and twisted half-around his waist. Both socks were tucked halfway into his shoes and his pants were only partially pulled up to his waist.

Tilley looked up at Bill as if he recognized him, but he didn't recognize him. When he turned onto his side, there was a stain at the back of his pants where he had urinated on himself and was laying on wet sheets. The smell almost made Bill gag and he thought he was going to vomit at one point when he saw a small brown smear on the elastic band of Tilley's underwear. Tilley's sheets were soaked in sweat. His pillow was greasy from the oils in his hair. There was a slight sheen of sweat on his face, too. Bill couldn't believe what he was seeing. Right before his eyes a man was totally breaking down both physically and mentally and there was nothing anyone could do about it.

Bill stared down at Tilley for a while longer before he moved any closer.

"Tilley. You look rough today. Do you want to take a shower or something?"

"I ain't gonna take no shower. I'm fine. My mother said I didn't have to take a bath but oncet a week on Saturday night and then I could sit in the tub with the birds and wash my feet and look up at the sky. I done took a bath last night. This old bed knocks and reels and rolls around in the middle of the night. Look there at them walls how they bow into the sides. This place is like a prison."

He wasn't making any sense whatsoever now.

Sammie came to the loft and stood at Bill's side. She held her hand over her face to keep the smell away from her nostrils. She turned her head in disgust.

"Isn't there anything we can do for him, Bill?" she whispered.

"I'm afraid not. He's his own guardian and the state won't let us force him into any type of treatment he doesn't want. We have to wait it out and see if we can convince him to take his medication. Maybe he'll get sick of living like this and clean himself up. We can't even make him take a shower

41

if he doesn't want to. The only thing we can do is send him out of here if he gets dangerous and tries to hurt himself or someone else. You know what that means. That would be the end of Tilley."

"I know but it seems so unfair. I just want to help him."

"Me, too, but we can't right now. It has to be his decision."

Bill had been warned that Tilley could get violent if he was pushed too much so he took caution to watch him closely. He watched Tilley a little longer, he took the plunge and decided to let him have it.

"Tilley, you're looking like you're sick and your space up here is a mess! It smells horrible. You're going to have to clean up or we'll have to call the doctor and get him over here to look at you! I mean it – shape up or ship out because that's what it's going to come to if a doctor comes over and see you like this!"

"I don't care about no doctor. I ain't afraid of no needles. They cain't hurt my mind and spirit and they cain't hurt my body neither. I'll just do like this and fight it off." Tilley attempted to raise his arm and make a muscle like a four-year-old does to impress his grandparents.

"Tilley, I don't want you to have to be hospitalized and go away. I'm afraid they might try to do something like you told me about before. Remember...?"

Reasoning at this point was probably useless but Bill had to try something to avoid the situation from escalating into something terrible. He hoped that the shock treatments he had experienced in the past were a strong enough reminder for the trouble that was lurking ahead.

"I ain't goin' to no hospital.! They cain't take me alive! They'll have to kill me first. I'm my own person and they cain't make me."

Tilley was screaming now which could spell danger. He was fully aware of his status as his own guardian. It had been drilled into his head so many times that he was practically an expert on the situation when he was rational.

"Tilley, if the doctor comes in to see you, he's going to recommend that you be hospitalized somewhere, and I know you don't want that to happen. Why don't you get out of bed and let me help you shave and clean up?"

Tilley laid there for a while longer and stared at the walls. This was something that had to be his own decision, and no one could help him make it. Bill also had to prepare himself for any necessary actions that might have to be taken which was something he didn't want to happen at all. Fed up, Bill let out a short sigh and turned to go away.

"Your decision, Tilley, it's up to you."

All Bill could do was wait to see if his speech had carried any results. Hopefully, Tilley would somehow be able to crawl down into the hole he had dug himself into and find a large enough piece of his own person to talk some sense into himself. If he did, the staff at Turkey Feather could get him cleaned up and a hot piece of meatloaf stuffed into his stomach (Hilda's specialty and Tilley's and Bill's favorite) and things would be fine in a day or so. If not, Tilley was headed for a psychiatric evaluation and a week at the local hospital where he would receive some major psychotropic medication to bring his functioning to a level that somewhat resembled normal. Tilley hated hospitals and would scratch and claw the doctors, the nurses, other patients, or anyone else who got in his way. Bill and the others who knew Tilley would have hated to have dealt with him at the hospital. It was amazing the strength someone with a mental illness could muster when they were "throwin' a fit" as Hilda would say. Bill had to agree, though, as he had seen enough heavy-duty shelving and tables sent flying across the room as a result of those "fits" to know they weren't fun to be around.

When Bill came back downstairs, Tina met him and asked how Tilley was.

"Not good. He looks like a mess."

"Hilda's makin' meatloaf today — that might get him in a better mood."

"Yep. We need all the help we can get right now. So, what are you doing right now?"

"Laundry. Want to help?"

"I think I remember something I had to do in the office."

"I see how ya are — laundry is woman's work, huh?"

"Now you know better than that. I really do have some things I need to do but maybe we can talk later."

"I hear ya."

In the office, Bill peered out the window at the leaves that were swirling from the ground. Standing there seemed to take him a thousand miles away into his own private world of daydreams and wishes. Bill thought about his life and what he wanted out of it. He thought about his family back home and his youth. He thought about all the things and all the people that he gave credit for making him who he was. Bill thought about Turkey Feather and all the things and people that had made the residents there who they were. So many stories were hidden down deep within their souls. There were stories that would never be told. There were stories that had never been told. All of them soon to be lost for eternity. Sadness, shame, laughter, and love were all mangled into a huge lump of history that would never be written. Not one ounce of glory in the whole blame thing.

As he stood there, Bill thought about the Quartet, too. He hadn't been suspicious of them much lately what with the season changing over to colder temperatures and the holidays coming on. They were pretty much subdued these past few weeks with Lester still recovering from his exhaustion attack. His potassium level dropped while he was in the hospital, and it was difficult for him to be overly active without tiring himself out after only a few minutes. Lester and the boys sat around and watched game shows, worked a bunch of crazy puzzles, and talked a lot about life, bragging to each other about all the things they had seen and done. It was good to listen to them from a distance and enjoy their camaraderie even if it was from arm's length.

In relation to the doom and gloom, the Quartet was truly an anomaly for Turkey Feather. These guys seemed to want to do something instead of giving up on life. They didn't let their spirits get broken by the doldrums of their environment. They tried to make some fun for themselves but, unfortunately, it was usually at the expense of Tina's and Sammie's rear ends. It was nice to know, though, that somewhere in their withering and aged bodies there was still something left that hadn't been squeezed out by life. Bill wished their zeal would have rubbed off on a few more of the other residents. It would have made things more interesting for sure.

"Hey, Bill. That boy is in there stinkin' up the place." Wilma must have seen me come out to the office earlier.

"Yeah, Wilma, I know. I had a talk with him earlier, but I don't know if it'll help any or not."

"Take and hose 'im down – that'll get him on the ball. 'at's what I'd do. We'll fix 'im."

"I might have to think about trying that, Wilma. I'll see what I can come up with. Say it's bad, huh?"

"Oh, yeah. He stinks up the whole place. He ain't fit for the buzzards to eat even."

"Well, that's bad, I guess. You been doin' all right, lately?"

"Oh, purty good I reckon. I ain't seen nobody out walkin' around at night none lately so I guess the bogeyman ain't comin' after me yet."

" Walkin' around at night? What do you mean?'

"Oh them boys in there go cattin' around sometimes all hours of the night. I reckon they're lookin' for somethin'."

"They do, huh? Wonder what they're lookin' for?"

"Beats me. Maybe they got a moonshine still or somethin'. My Daddy used to make moonshine sometimes and he'd be out all night long. My Momma though he had 'im a girlfriend 'til she follored 'im one night and seen what he was doin'. Then she told 'im if he didn't give her some of the money, she'd tell on 'im for it. He made her help him from then on."

"Sounds fair enough, I guess. Wilma, you ever see those boys you were talking about doing anything else suspicious?"

"What boys? Them little fellers up the holler? They play way too close to the road, I tell ya that much."

Damn. She was fading just as Bill almost had another clue.

"I fussed at 'em and they throwed rocks at me. I grabbed one of 'em up and busted his little ass before his Mommy come down and cussed me for it. I let her have it, too. I knocked her glasses clean off her nose and left her layin' there in the dirt. Them little bastards was throwin' rocks at me like that. They boys was downright little bastards. That's fer sure. She'd had ever man in the county."

"Wilma, the boys have been walking around at night, you said. What do they do? Do you ever hear what they're saying?"

"Oh, I don't know what they's doin. They's just little fellers even if they are mean as Hell. They don't do much cause they's too little, ya know, and they cain't talk so's you can understand what they're sayin'."

It looked like she had slipped away for sure. It was no use badgering her, so Bill told Wilma he hoped she had a nice day and to behave herself. She winked and grinned and assured him she would be a good girl. Yeah, right.

What Wilma told Bill confirmed his worries. The Quartet had been slipping around at night as part of their little quest, had they? That meant they were putting themselves in further danger given what the forest around Nickleville held in store for unsuspecting hikers. Enough was enough at this point so it was time for a showdown with the guys. Bill would put Sammie, Tina, and Frank, and even Hilda, on full alert if he had to just to keep an eye out. The last thing Bill needed was to have someone get lost in the woods late at night or to slip down into one of the caves around Turkey Feather. It wouldn't have been the first time it had happened. Those four might be feeble but they were up to no good. He was sure of that.

CHAPTER THREE

Bill sat down at the desk and looked over some more paperwork for a couple of hours before calling it an early day and heading home. He was determined to find something in the books he had checked out that would help him with his own search. The problem was Bill had no idea what he would be looking for or even what he might think would be interesting enough to consider a possibility. Turkey Feather was chock full of possibilities and the place had a life all its own. There was always that magic that Bill felt about it, though. Just when the days seemed darkest and you thought there was no reason to go on hoping for anything better, Turkey Feather managed to hit a straight stretch in life's highway and things always leveled out. Even the residents seemed to have an uncanny ability to pull a rabbit out of their hats when it came to their health or their finances or even their own personalities when they got depressed or disheartened. Something funny would manage to lift their spirits or a stray cat would make its way down from Lucy's, do a few cute tricks for everyone, and then mosey back up the drive. Turkey Feather was a special place and Bill believed they all sensed an invisible protective presence there. It almost felt as if God himself had taken pity on Turkey Feather and came by to check on things and make it all better. Bill was sure He must have felt bad about the differences He had planned for their lives and the courses of actions that had transpired for some of them.

Then there was the issue with Claudia. She never changed. She had managed to survive be it by sheer determination or being blessed with good health, but she only took it one day at a time. Unfortunately, no attempt at unlocking her deepest secrets or memories ever prevailed so Bill had to piece her history together with what he had found in her file. Fortunately, although it was a small file, it had quality papers and pictures that were taken before and after her Holocaust experience. The few papers that were in the file written in another language that appeared to be German. It wasn't in any kind of order, but it was enough to get a small picture of how her life had evolved. She and her sister suffered severe tortures, but her sister had managed somehow to take care of them both.

Claudia's stay at Turkey Feather was unusual at best. The Sherlock Holmes game Bill was being forced to play was quickly getting old. He needed solid answers about some serious issues. If he didn't get those answers soon, something was going to happen. Bill had yet to find anything to confirm where her finances came from. No bank statements, no documentation of a payee, no guardianship…nothing. The only thing that looked like a financial statement was a document printed in that same foreign language, but he still had no clue as to what it could be, only suspicions. There were numbers but not in any format or sequence that he recognized so they were useless until he could find someone who could read it all. How were they getting paid for her? There had to be something somewhere. As bad as he hated to do it, Bill was going to have to call Mr. Rounder to find out more about Claudia. He was afraid that would pry into some areas that neither Rounder, nor Bill, wanted to visit. There was simply no other way at this point, though. Bill would make the call first thing in the morning. Right now, he was going to plop down and look through his history books some more.

History has an amazing ability to keep tiny secrets from us. It also has an amazing ability to reveal the slightest details that have seemingly escaped our notice even when the object is right in front of our eyes the whole time. Bill flipped through a half-dozen or so of the references on Nickleville and the region around it hopelessly looking for that slight detail that would enlighten him, that pearl of great price, that magic lantern with which to open the golden door to Ali Baba's treasure. He was sure he would be able to find what he was looking for but where? Bill read and flipped and scanned and perused and then, like the proverbial needle in a haystack, there it was. The answer to his mystery. A single newspaper picture taken decades ago that explained it all in six sentences. Lester was even quoted as him and his crew planning a trip to Ocean Beach near San Diego, California, maybe, to retire when everything was done. Bill couldn't believe it. He also couldn't believe the boys had been involved with something like this for so long. What were they thinking? Did they know what they were doing? Even worse, what if they knew exactly what they were getting themselves into and knew exactly what they were doing? These guys had been around one another for a lifetime. Turkey Feather was no happenstance for them.

Now that Bill knew of the glue holding the Quartet together, he had some thinking to do. Lucky for him there was plenty of time to do that at Turkey Feather. He had to formulate a plan. He needed reinforcements and he had to figure out a way to approach the Quartet so as not to spook them. Bill had to gain their full and complete trust. If he made a mistake, they would bolt for the door, and all would be lost. Bill thought about asking Sammy and Tina to help but even that would be risky. Too many people meant too many chances to blab the secret to everyone. The boys had been working on this for a long time and would be extra suspicious of anything out of the ordinary. They were professionals all right. They knew what they were doing, too. Bill was just afraid that taking on the four of them would be a bigger task than he realized. Frank's assistance was a possibility, but Bill knew he was busy outside of Turkey Feather. He wouldn't want to spend much more time there than necessary. It looked like it was going to be left to Bill to figure it out on his own for now. This was going to be extremely interesting to say the least.

Armed with new and powerful information, Bill went to work on his plan in his spare time. He knew the boys had been scheming for a while, but he fancied himself a pretty good schemer, too. Bill went back and forth to the libraries all around Nickelville to gather as many facts as possible. He would need everything he could get his hands on to catch up with the boys. He copied pictures and all sorts of maps of the area and compiled them into a nice, neat portfolio worthy of presentation. After a couple of weeks, he was ready. Confident that he could handle things on his own, Bill headed up the showdown by himself.

The Quartet was working their "crossword puzzles" when Bill walked in. He knew they were intent on their work by the way they shuffled their pages and tried to cover them up as nonchalantly as possible.

"Howdy, boys!" Bill grinned from ear-to-ear.

Lester raised his head up slowly and nodded like he was too tired to speak.

"Uh…howdy, Bill" Mavis said cautiously.

"Fellas – I have something for you to look at. It's a little piece I've been working on for a few weeks or so about the history of this area. Not being from around here, I thought it would be good for me to familiarize myself with the place. You boys take a good look and let me know what you think. Let's just keep it between us right now because I don't want anyone seeing it until I'm ready. Never know – I might want to write a book about it one day."

With that, Bill plopped the file down on the table and smiled at each one of the boys before turning to walk away. Just as he reached the door of the dining area, he turned back to the Quartet.

"I'll be in my office when you're ready to give your critique."

The Quartet sat there for a minute taking turns staring at one another. Lester hesitantly reached out for the file and focused his full attention on it. As he picked it up, he gave the rest of the Quartet a solemn stare. Each of them looked back at Lester with equal interest. They knew they had been caught.

Lester opened the file. He looked at the first page and dropped his head.

"What is it?" Fred asked in a whisper.

Lester raised his face and sighed. He placed the newspaper photograph of the four of them taken forty-six years ago on the table for the others to see.

"He knows. That's what it is."

"I told you we shouldn't have come here."

Mavis burst unto the conversation.

"What are we going to do?"

Lester looked at him and shot back.

"We'll meet with him is what we're going to do."

"But Les…we can't. He'll want everything for himself."

Raymond could have had a point, but it was too late now.

"I don't think so, Raymond. If he did, why would he give us this file? He could have taken the information in it and went out on his own. I think he's giving us a chance to come clean and that's what we're going to have to do. If we don't and we cause him too much grief, he'll go to the Feds and we'll lose everything. Let's go talk to him right now."

Lester took the file in his hands as he stood up. He placed his finger to his lips and locked eyes with each of them to make sure they kept quiet. They marched out of the dining room like a gang of undercover agents on a mission. Not even Hilda asked them their business when they walked past. They all crammed into the building as best as possible. Given the sneaky grin on his face, Bill had been waiting for this moment for a good while.

"Well, boys, that didn't take too long. Glad you could join me." Bill motioned for them to sit and they squeezed into what space they could find.

"How did you find out?" Lester began.

"I guess I'm just nosey."

"Nosey? Hmph! How'd you find out? One of us told, that's how! Which one of ya squealed?"

Raymond pointed his finger around the room and looked at his comrades with disdain.

"RAYMOND! Get hold of yourself! No one told me a thing. I figured it out on my own, I told you. You guys always going on your trips, walking around here with a bunch of papers, acting all suspicious all the time. It wasn't that difficult to realize something was up."

"Look, Sonny, that treasure is ours and no one is gonna take it from us."

Mavis was showing a side of the Quartet Bill had never seen before.

"Hold on there, Mavis. I'm not here to take anything from you. You don't have to be so mean about it. Sheesh!"

Lester spoke.

"Well, what are you up to? You obviously know the value of what we're looking for or you wouldn't have gathered us in here. We don't mean to get nasty, Bill, but you need to realize we've been working on this for years. Long before we came to Turkey Feather."

"I know. I read the article about it. Nice picture by the way. It took me a while to put all the information together. At first, it was hard to make any sense of it all, but it finally came around. Didn't you fellas think you would ever be found out? What did you think you were going to do if you found anything? How were you going to handle that?"

Bill leaned back in his chair to give them a chance to answer.

"We've already found it," Fred said matter-of-factly.

"DAMMIT, Fred! Keep your mouth shut."

Bill's eyes widened.

"Already?"

"Let me explain." Lester raised his hand and gestured the room to be quiet.

"It's not that simple, Bill. Fred gets excited and carried away some when we talk about it. We've been looking for so long, that it's become an obsession for us. It hasn't been easy to keep quiet either. When we were younger, as you probably know from your little research file there, we were called treasure hunters and land pirates. People around these parts just laughed at us and teased us about looking for fool's gold or the Loch Ness Monster or something ridiculous like that. Back then, people didn't understand. I guess we didn't, either, because we were too young. To us, it was more than treasure hunting or riches or anything like that. It was about accomplishments. Everybody thought we were a bunch of cracked pots. After a while, we almost started to believe what they were saying ourselves. We looked for the treasure for years and, to this day, we've never given up. Oh, the newspapers and TV stations used to come around and talk to us when they needed a human-interest piece, but they all treated us like we were looking for a UFO or a Bigfoot. We wanted to be remembered – respected for something other than being a bunch of kooks. We got tired of all the negative publicity and a little spooked that someone might take us seriously and cut in on our hunt, so we cooled it for a while. We even disbanded to keep people from asking us about it and getting ideas of their own. Months turned into years and years turned into a couple decades before we tried it again. By that point, our families had all pretty much left us over our obsession and all we had left was each other. Then, the best possible thing in the world happened."

Bill was on the edge of his seat by now and hung on Lester's every word. He whispered two words.

"Turkey Feather."

Lester smiled.

"Exactly. Turkey Feather. Somehow, the gods smiled down on us, and Turkey Feather was opened as an old folks' home. We couldn't believe our luck. We were in need of a place like Turkey Feather, and it seemed like fate, so we jumped at the chance to come here. We pooled our resources and transferred everything over to charities to put ourselves into abject poverty and away we went. You see, Bill, what Fred means when he says we've already found our treasure is that we think the treasure is here at Turkey Feather."

"Here?" Bill's eyebrows raised so high they made his forehead hurt.

"Yes. We think there is a treasure of some sort buried here at Turkey Feather."

"Yeah – and it's all ours, too," Raymond interjected.

Mavis patted Raymond on the arm to quiet him.

"It's okay, Raymond. I think we might have another treasure hunter in our midst. Look at that gleam in his eye."

As Lester and Fred leaned forward, Mavis shifted his weight into Bill.

"Yep, I think you might be right," Mavis whispered.

Bill placed his elbows on his desk and looked around the room.

"I don't know about all that, boys. I stay busy around here and don't have time for a bunch of treasure hunting nonsense. I mean – not that it's nonsense. It's just hard to believe that this old place was a haven for pirates or has a treasure chest hidden somewhere."

"You can't look at it like that, Billy Boy. You've got to believe in something and then it becomes different than some story. It becomes a part of you. A lot of folks have hobbies or jobs that they devote their entire lives to. Then, one day, they wake up and it's all gone. That's what happened to us, too. We've lost our families and friends and put everything we own up for hock just to pursue some crazy dream. If you stop dreaming, Bill, you die. This is what keeps us going."

Fred had a point. He was usually quieter so that gave his statement even more weight. Bill sat there and looked at the faces of each member of the Quartet. So much had been given up by each of them and, still, they had hope. How could a person tell them to stop looking for something or doing something that was the essence of their existence? Bill knew he didn't have the heart to tell them to stop searching.

"Fellas, I'm not going to stop you. I don't think anyone could stop you. That wouldn't be right to do that to you. Not when you've put so much into this. I'll tell you what I can do, though, if you promise not to go at it too hard, I can send Frank with you sometimes to help. That way someone will be with you in case somebody has another exhaustion attack or something."

Fred almost came out of his seat.

"Good God, man! No way would we let Frank, or anybody else, come along!"

"That's the deal, guys. I can't afford to lose one of you on an excursion and that's final."

"It's not fair. That treasure is ours and nobody is gonna take it from us."

Lester looked at the others and they all nodded together in silence. Then they looked back at Bill.

"How about you come along instead of Frank? How would that be?"

"Oh no…you're not going to get me to come with you. I've got too much to do here, and besides, I don't have a clue what I'm looking for."

"We do. Whoever left this thing here, hid the clues in plain sight. You wouldn't believe all the stuff we've found just layin; around inside. Clues that were right in front of everyone's eyes, but nobody paid any attention to them. One of the biggest clues we found was hangin' in the house."

"Hanging in the house? Why would anyone hang a clue to a treasure in plain sight of the whole world?"

"Purely psychological, my boy – the more important an item is, the easier it is to hide it in plain view. See that cross-stitch tapestry on the wall behind you?"

Bill turned around and looked at a faded cross-stitch pattern on the wall. The layer of dust had faded the piece to the point that it almost blended into the wall. Bill had never noticed it hanging there before now.

"That thing? I thought it was some leftover craft item somebody left."

Lester explained.

"We did, too, until we found some information in a journal that we managed to get our hands on. It was a journal written by the wife of Captain

Tiberius J. Fink. Captain Fink was rumored to be the very one who had stolen the gold shipment. A few years ago, this place had to have some work done on it. They tore the well house down and left the debris lying around for a few days. Naturally, we all poked around after the workers left in the evenings. Luckily, we found the journal tucked down in a corner of the foundation. It was water-worn but salvageable."

"He was a fink by nature as well as by name, the Captain was." Mavis jabbed.

"Captain Fink's wife wrote in her journal about him helping her with her cross-stitches after he came back from the war. She said she thought he was doing it for relaxation purposes to keep his mind off the tragedies he had witnessed. Oddly, he would only work on the cross-stitch patterns alone. She mentioned in the entries that she was worried about him because he would often mumble while he worked. She wrote how she felt he was possessed by a being or spirit that was drawing him away from her. The journal entries also mentioned that Captain Fink also spent many, many hours staring off into the wilderness with a wild gleam in his eye. Mrs. Fink thought he had met another woman while he was away at war. Little did she know, the mysterious lover was the gold her husband had killed for. Another thing she didn't know was that the tapestry the Captain had created revealed the keys to this precious fortune. Captain Fink had cleverly stitched a short poem and flowers into the fabric that would serve as a reminder to him. A reminder of where the gold was hidden. Apparently, the gold lust was taking hold of his mind and causing him to lose his memory. Or maybe it was the guilt that constantly gnawed at him that made him go crazy. Whatever it was, Captain Fink left the clues in the tapestry for a reason. The poem revealed something about the treasure that no one would ever suspect. Look at it and tell me what it says."

Bill looked at Lester for a second like he didn't believe him. Lester nodded his head for him to go ahead and try. Bill turned toward the tapestry. He lifted it from its nail and blew some dust off the top of the frame. He sat back down and looked closely at the piece. Bill cleared his throat and read the words aloud.

> *By hand is made the rooted hollow.*
>
> *While fortune slumbers, shame shall follow.*
>
> *Through weeping pane, the wealth does reveal*
>
> *The burden's haunting does remain still.*

Wisdom lacks for the branch's training,

The secret deepens at the raining.

Alas, the darkness shall fill my soul,

To rid the guilty and make me whole.

The room fell silent. Bill raised his head to look at the others. They were all grinning with a quizzical look in their eye.

"Okay. You got me. What the heck does it all mean?"

"That's what we had hoped you could help us with."

Lester clasped his hands and peered into Bill's eyes with an encouraging stare as if he were trying to help Bill come up with an answer.

"Honestly, fellas, I don't have a clue. I mean it does sound like there's something out there somewhere, but it doesn't mention anything about where, or what it is, or anything else for that matter."

Mavis raised his arms up over his head and shook his hands for affect.

"It doesn't matter, Bill, what it is – you don't understand."

Bill looked saddened at Mavis. At that moment, he finally realized just how much this all meant to Mavis and the rest of the men.

"No, Mavis, I'm afraid I don't understand. I'm sorry."

Mavis sighed and hung his head.

Lester took over at that point.

"You see, Bill, it's not so important what the treasure is as much as it's important that it's found. To tell the truth about it, it's not even so much that it's important that it's found as that we're the ones that find it. We've given up our whole lives for this. We've lost everything – our families, our friends, our careers – even a part of ourselves to the pursuit of this thing that we don't even know what it is. We're old now and we need a reason to keep going. When you get our age, you'll understand. Each of us here with you right now is looking for a chance at immortality. A chance to go down in history. Sometimes, people just can't be happy with what they were blessed with in life. They waste a whole lifetime looking for that something that will make them rich or give them some measure of happiness they think will sustain them forever. Unfortunately, it was too late for us to turn it all around. We finally figured out that the happiness we had searched for was right there in front of our eyes. It was in our families and friends. We wasted it all for a dream that turned into a nightmare. That's why this is so important to us now. It's our last hope at redemption and we need you to help us."

After a speech like that, Bill was choked up. He looked deeply into the eyes of the old men before him. He thought about all the things they had given up for a pipe dream and felt so sorry for them that he could barely fight the tears back.

Fred looked up at Bill and whispered to him like a child would to a parent.

"Please help us, Bill, before it's too late."

"Yeah, Bill, please help us," Raymond said as he held out his hand for Bill to confirm his assistance.

"I don't know, guys, I…I…"

Lester stood up and placed his hand over Raymond's. Fred and Mavis followed suit. All four of them were looking at Bill with their hands layered in unison.

Bill shook his head and hesitantly placed his hand on top of the stack of gnarled and knotty digits.

"Awww…Hell…how can a guy turn you bunch of con artists down?"

The Quartet broke into laughter and their faces lit up like kids at Christmas.

"Now don't tell a soul, Bill. You're the only one we've trusted with this secret for nearly fifty years. We don't want to blow it now."

"I know all about confidentiality. I even took a class on it in college about it once, but I never thought I'd be using it regarding buried treasure or whatever it is we're looking for."

Lester held up his finger like a candlestick and hunched his shoulders in excitement.

"That's the next step, my boy. We've got to figure out what it is we're looking for exactly. We have an idea, but we've never been able to confirm anything. That tapestry is the closest thing we've ever found that linked us to a solid, iron-clad clue."

"Yeah – now that we know how good you are at research, you can help us figure out the rest of it, right Les?"

"Right, Mavis. You're going to be our new crypto man. You're in charge of solving that riddle and figuring out more clues. We believe we've put together enough to keep you busy for a while so get ready."

"Ready. Yeah, right. I don't think there is any 'ready' with you guys."

Fred narrowed his eyes in persistence.

"Don't be so hard on us, Bill, just get into the spirit of things and help us."

"I'm not trying to be hard on you, Fred, I just can't believe that I agreed to this."

Raymond slapped him on his back surprisingly hard for a man of his age.

"Don't lose faith, Bill, we're almost there."

Each member of the Quartet threw in a round of their own encouragement and headed out the door to leave Bill with his thoughts. He looked over at the tapestry one more time and read it again. He almost knew he wouldn't sleep until he figured it out. Bill was a definite type-A personality, and this thing could conceivably drive him insane before any resolve came from it. Nevertheless, he straightened his shoulders and promised himself he would see the Quartet through with their dream. He couldn't turn his back on them now.

A couple of days passed before Bill saw much of the Quartet again. The guys were professionals at keeping things low-key. After all, they had done this sort of thing for almost five decades. Bill found himself looking all over Turkey Feather for clues. Sudden, he looked at the mundane objects and contours of Turkey Feather a little different. Even the residents seemed to look different. Bill knew this could weigh very heavily on his mind, so he tried to guard himself against obsessing over it. The Quartet had done enough of that already for anyone else who might ever aspire to their dream.

A few days after the showdown with the Quartet, Bill was sitting at the archive film projector in the library at Beech Knoll. He caught a glimpse of someone familiar out of the corner of his eye. It was Sammie. She was with another young woman, and they were looking through a pile of books. She hadn't seen him, so he quickly put his papers and microfiche films away and returned them to the reference desk. He walked over to an aisle of books and stared through the hardbacks to get a closer look at Sammie and her friend.

He couldn't quite hear what they were saying but he thought he heard them discussing Sammie's options. Bill looked at the pile of books on the table and saw the letters 'G.E.D.' on the spine of one. He looked closer. Another book had the word 'Algebra' and still another 'English' in the titles. Sammie must be talking to her friend about going back to school and getting her GED like she had told him when they first met. Bill was pleased to see Sammie taking some initiative. He decided not to take a chance on embarrassing her and slipped out of the library without interrupting her. Even if Bill didn't find anything on Turkey Feather that day, he was impressed with what he saw out of Sammie.

From the point of the showdown on, Bill and the Quartet tried to meet on a semi-regular basis to discuss their progress. They called it their "man's meetings" but if people only knew what they were up to they probably would have run them out of Turkey Feather. The boys had pretty much exhausted their cache of clues and Bill wasn't finding anything in the papers at the libraries. He had even contacted the local historical society to see if he could find any information. Bill used a "new to the area" disguise as the lead-in to discussion about Civil War activity in the area. Nothing much about treasure, though. Mostly a few battles in some of the surrounding areas. It was frustrating for him and the Quartet to know they were close to finding something but none of them had an idea as to what they might find or how. They just knew it would be soon. They all had a feeling.

The Quartet and Bill slowed their treasure hunt down for a few weeks and played along with the holiday spirits. Thanksgiving was passing and the Christmas season was fast upon them. Turkey Feather was bustling with a little excitement that year. Bill had Sammie and Tina buy some nice decorations for all the rooms and Santa hats for the staff. They wore the hats like good little elves and the residents were as thrilled as little kids to see all the festivities. Church groups had poured in with fruit baskets, fruit cakes, fruit cookies, and fruity preachers and carolers. The local hot dog hot spot even donated lunch one day which thrilled Tilley to no end. The last count anyone took he had eaten five and probably snatched a few more to take to his room.

To make things even more lively, the girls came up with an idea to host a Christmas party for the residents complete with a dance and punch and music. Bill wasn't so sure it was a great idea, but he went along with it when Sammie batted her eyes and said, "Pleeeaaassseee, Bill...pwetty pwease..."and pouted her bottom lip out at him. He was sure she was flirting now, and he couldn't say no to such a shameless show of intentional mischief.

The party was kept a secret until the big day, and no one suspected a thing until Sammie and Tina gathered everyone in the dining room just after breakfast and let everyone know there would be a big surprise that night. They all smiled and chattered when they found out about the secret and Wilma clasped her hands together beaming as wide as her mouth would allow.

"Santa Claus is comin' to town!" she exclaimed.

The whole place erupted in laughter. It was a sign that there was still a lot of life in those old bones and what seemed like a drawer full of dull utensils was really a drawer full of sharp knives just waiting for the chance to be used again. Somehow, some way, those residents had come alive and were happy again. Bill never thought it was possible to see so much life at Turkey Feather. He guessed the folks there just needed some encouragement and a chance to let it all out. Maybe Bill and the girls had it all wrong. Maybe all that Turkey Feather needed was a little touch of love and excitement to breathe life into the residents once again. Maybe they just needed a reason to live again. Either way, the Christmas surprise Sammie and Tina promised was sure the talk of Turkey Feather that day.

The girls had gone all out and planned a huge production. They enlisted the help of the usual volunteers to coordinate crafts and bingo while they wrapped the donated gifts they had gathered. There had never been so many soaps and lotions and cologne float through Turkey Feather. Hilda and Frank got in on the action, too, and had the whole place lit up and smelling like gingerbread cookies. It seemed like the only one who didn't have a role in the whole party plan was Bill. Unfortunately for Bill, Sammie and Tina had thought of a job for him, too.

"Hey Bill...whatcha doin?"

Sammie was looking at him with her head cocked to the side like she was waiting for him to try to lie his way out of something. She was right.

"Well, nothing right now but I have a lot to do a little later."

"Uh huh...I see. I guess I'm gonna have to do this the hard way."

"What do you mean, the "hard way"?

"Oh, YOU'LL see, you'll see…"

"I don't like the sound of that. What do you have in mind?"

Sammie motioned with her finger for Bill to come toward her.

"Just trust me…"

Hesitating, Bill walked toward Sammie as she took his hand to lead him outside.

"Now listen, Bill Handley. You and I both now this party won't be complete unless Santa shows…"

"OH NO! Not me! I am NOT playing Santa Claus! Out of the question…"

"BILL! Shame on you! Tina and I have done all this work and the least you could do is to appease us with this one request. Besides, I promise I'll make it worth your while."

"What do you mean by that?"

"Oh, I'm sure you wouldn't pass up a nice pecan pie or a fruit cake made from scratch, now would ya?"

"How'd you know pecan pie was my favorite?"

"I figured. ALL men like pecan pie. It's just their nature"

"Whole pecans and not the little pieces crumbled up?"

"Whole pecans. If you do a good job, I might even find a surprise for you if you're a good boy."

"What do…"

"Shhh…now hurry up and get to your office and put the suit on."

"There's no suit in there!"

"There is now! Now hurry up!"

"Why you little…I oughta…"

Sammie winked.

"Yes, you should but that will have to wait until later."

"Uh...oookkkaaayyy..."

Bill smiled and went to the office like a good boy. Who was he to go against orders and pecan pie and maybe some other surprise? He'd just have to play jolly old St. Nick for a little while and the residents would love it. Secretly, Bill was honored and thrilled that he had been chosen to play Santa. He grinned from ear to ear while he donned the big red suit.

When he was ready, Bill stepped out onto the patio and waited for Sammie and Tina. To his surprise, they were dressed as twin elves. He laughed when he saw them, and Tina had to settle him down.

"Dang it, Santa! Don't you know you have to be quiet before your big entrance?"

Bill stifled a laugh.

"Oh, oh...okay...I'll be quiet...".

"Sammie, you wait with Santa, and I'll go see what everybody is doing. Project Secret Santa is underway!"

Sammie smiled wide.

"I can handle that!"

Bill looked at her and rolled his eyes. She was so blatant these days with her flirting.

Just as Tina left Bill and Sammie, Sammie pointed to the top of the door facing.

"Well, would you look at that. A mistletoe. You know what that means."

Bill shot a scowl at her.

"Of course, I know what that means, silly. We don't have time for foolishness. Santa has a job to do and so do his elves. Besides, what would people say if they saw you kissing Santa."

Sammie started to sing.

"Santa Cutie, and hurry down the chimney tonight…"

"Oh, good grief…would you stop that?!"

Sammie leaned into Bill and looked up into his eyes with a goofy grin.

"What's wong, Santy…is da Santy Cutie shy…"

"You are IMPOSSIBLE tonight! Have you been in the egg nog already?"

"Maybe, Santy…maybe I want to get into more than the egg nog…"

While Bill and Sammie were outside bantering back and forth, they didn't notice the commotion inside.

Apparently, Claudia had escaped again and made her way to the party. Unbeknownst to anyone, she had entered the dining room and found a seat between the tree and the stack of presents the volunteers brought. She sat there quietly while she took it all in. Smiling. Claudia was smiling. Not a single soul noticed her until the First Baptist choir gathered around the piano to sing carols. They began to sing "The Fist Noel" and then, out of nowhere, much to everyone's utter amazement and complete astonishment, the little shriveled and wrinkled demoniac stood up all by herself and raised her arms as if to conduct her own personal symphony. What happened next was nothing short of a miracle.

Claudia began to sing. Not just any singing. This was real singing. Not quite opera but way more than a choir. It was certainly a trained voice that was coming out of that scrawny and bedraggled body. No one could believe what they were witnessing. Claudia had quite a reputation and even the regular volunteers who came to Turkey Father knew all about her outbursts and fits. The room went silent for a second until the pianist had the wherewithal to keep playing. The sound was amazing and beautiful, and everyone began to tear up. Claudia's voice rang out strong and true. She was singing the song in German and even though no one could understand what she was saying, they knew the voice of an angel was gently brushing their ears and transforming the hearts of everyone in the room.

"What the heck is taking so long?" Bill said in frustration.

"This suit is getting hot."

"Oh now, Santy's elf has got Santy all hot and bothered."

"STOP IT, you nut!"

Sammie and Bill both laughed. Just then, Bill glanced up to see everyone staring at something. He couldn't' see what they were looking at, so he moved closer to the window.

"*Whatthe...?*"

"What is it, Santy?"

Bill pointed inside.

"LOOK!"

"Oh...my...God..."

Sammie's eyes widened and her mouth hung wide. She placed her hand on the window and stood in amazement.

Bill nudged her.

"Come on. Let's go inside!"

Santa Claus Bill, and Sammie the Elf, were falling over one another as they scrambled to get inside and check out what neither of them, nor anyone else, could believe.

When they rushed in, Tina looked at them in total disbelief. Her eyes were as wide as her entire face, and she stood there frozen by the beauty of the moment. Sammie gave her the same look and just shrugged her shoulders and raised her eyebrows.

"*Whatthe...?*" she silently mouthed to Tina.

Claudia was waving her arms in rhythm to the sound the piano made. Fortunately, the pianist was classically trained, too, and knew what to do. She was leading the pianist as the song progressed and it was more wonderful than they could all bear. Most all of the ladies were weeping, and the men stood with their heads hung down knowing that what they were hearing was not of this world. This was indeed a miraculous moment they knew they would never witness again.

At the close of the song, silence fell over the room, and no one stirred. Claudia then amazed her crowd once more by dancing a waltz of sorts. There was no music and only Claudia was dancing. The smile on her face said to everyone witnessing this spectacle that she was at complete peace. No one had ever seen her smile more or look as happy. All anyone at Turkey Feather had ever seen out of Claudia was ranting and screaming and fighting. Even her appearance seemed to glow as if she had finally taken some pride in her grooming and had something to look nice for.

The pianist watched Claudia closely and began to play a slow tune that matched Claudia's movement. Bill had heard it before and knew the song to be "Fur Elise" which was one of his favorites. Tears welled in Bill's eyes and streamed down his cheeks. He had never seen something so beautiful and mesmerizing in his life. He stood there in awe of the miracle of Claudia's movements and joy.

Finally, after Claudia had danced enough, she sat down in a heap in the middle of the floor. Apparently, she had tired herself to the point of exhaustion. She sat with her head hung over not moving. After what seemed like a brief eternity, Tina went over to Claudia and touched her shoulder.

Claudia didn't move.

Tina shook her gently.

Claudia lifted her head and looked Tina in the eyes. In a garbled voice, Claudia managed to get a few words out in simple format.

"Thanky for let me dance."

She laid her head down against her chest again and let out a heavy sign. She slumped into Tina and closed her eyes. Tina placed her arms around her and held her tightly as if to let her know everything was alright. She looked across at Bill and Sammie and motioned with her head for them to come over to her and Claudia.

Bill and Sammie gathered themselves and knelt beside Claudia and Tina. The three of them rose together and lifted her to her feet. As they took her to her room to put her back to bed, Bill nodded to Frank and Hilda to keep the party going and get everyone back on track with the festivities.

When they made it to Claudia's bed, they tried the best they could to handle the weight of her body hanging from their shoulders. Once they had managed to dump her into her bed as softly as possible, they covered her up and stood back to quietly watch her.

Bill broke the silence.

"Ol' gal had quite a night tonight."

Tina looked at Bill.

"She sure did. While you two were outside, you should have seen the faces of the people from the church. You'd have thought Jesus Himself was standin' in the middle of the room. I think Hilda 'bout had a cow."

Sammie laughed.

"I'd say so. I couldn't believe it, either. Me and Bill kept wonderin' what the hold-up was."

"She looks tired. Let's go back and just leave her here for now. You two girls can check on her later tonight or in the morning and see how she is."

"Okay. I'll check on her after the party and see how she is then."

"Thanks, Tina. Sammie, I think we better get in there and do our Santa and Elf bit."

"Oh, yes sir, Santa, Sir."

Bill furrowed his brow at her.

"Now don't you go startin' that stuff again."

The three of them laughed at the merriment and Tina said something that gave Sammie and Bill both reason to pause.

"You two are cute together."

With that Sammie and Bill both blushed as red as Rudolph's shiny nose and both of them looked straight down at the floor.

"Uh…come on, Sammie, I think we better go hand out some gifts."

"Why are you two blushin' so bad? Hmmm…I must have hit a nerve."

Sammie half-squealed at Tina.

"SHAME ON YOU!"

Tina shrugged her shoulders and walked past Sammie and Bill.

"Just sayin'…"

Bill looked at Sammie. They both smiled for a fleeting second and headed back to the party. Everyone as talking about Claudia and her performance. All the residents asked how she was doing and if she was sick. Bill assured everyone that she was fine in his best Santa voice and the party resumed.

Sammie the Elf took her place beside Santa Claus Bill and helped hand out gifts. Each of the residents received their wrapped gift like a child. They handled it so delicately and treated it as if it were a precious gem. To many of them, it was the first gift they'd received in a long time, and they seemed to want to savor the experience for as long as possible. Some of them meticulously removed the wrapping paper and bows or ribbons while others tore into theirs like children. It was a bittersweet moment to see the joy of the present and the sadness of Christmas past meld into one.

Everyone ate and drank the booze-free punch and the music played and played. Some even expected to see Claudia in a repeat performance and, secretly, everyone would have been fine with her interrupting things again. When it was time for the volunteers to go, they hugged the residents and bid them farewell encouraging them to have a Merry Christmas. The magic of the spirit of Christmas had brought Turkey feather alive if for just one night and what a night it was. Word of this party would be talked about for years to come. So it was at Turkey Feather, the first Christmas that Bill Handley spent there. Things had been up and down for most of the year, but they all turned out right for Christmas at least.

The next morning, Bill got a phone call at home.

"Hello. Yes, Sammie what is it?"

"It's Claudia. She isn't responding and she's cold. Get here as quick as you can."

"I'll be right there."

Bill jumped out of bed and threw on the clothes he had worn underneath the Santa suit the night before. He raced the Mustang to Turkey Feather at breakneck speed. There was a thin sheen of frozen glaze on the driveway and Bill slid his back wheels coming around the last turn.

He popped out of the car and slammed the door. "Heeeyyy…better watch out. 'Em policemen are gonna take you to jail drivin' fast like that…"

Tilley was standing in Bill's way at the front door with a huge smile and a cigarette hanging in his mouth. Apparently, he had forgiven Bill for his outburst weeks ago and the Christmas party last night had put all the residents in a great mood. Bill was careful to handle Tilley carefully this time.

"You're right, Sheriff Tilley. I better watch out. I need to go inside to check on some things so, why you give the place a look-over and see if anything is going on around here."

"Sheriff?!?! Gosh, that makes me special!"

"That's right, Sheriff. Now go see if you can round up any wrongdoers."

"Yes, SIR! I will!"

Tilley saluted Bill and flicked his cigarette into the shrubs. He turned and walked away like a man on a mission.

Bill went to Claudia's room and stood in the doorway.

Lucy was sitting beside Claudia's bed with tears streaming down her face. Tina was holding Claudia's hand. She walked over to Bill.

"She's gone. I guess last night must have been too much for her."
"Has anyone called an ambulance?"

"Sammie is now."

"Okay. Where is she?

"She had to call from Lucy's place. Your office was locked, and the phone here must have been knocked off the charger cause it's dead."

Tina caught her words. She teared up and raised her head to Bill.

"I mean…"

"It's fine. I know what you meant. It's okay. You go on and take care of Claudia's things

and try to fix her up before she goes out. I'll find Sammie."

Bill went out to look for Sammie. When he got to Lucy's place, he could hear her talking inside.

"Yes, that's right. Claudia Saltzmann."She spelled it out for the dispatcher, thanked her, and hung the phone up.

Bill heard her whimpering through the door. He knocked gently and waited for her reply.

"Who is it?"

"It's me. Bill."

He heard her get up to unlock the door. When she opened the door, her hair and make-up were both a mess. It looked like she had been up all night.

"Hey. When did you get here?"

"A few minutes ago."

"Oh, Bill…"

Sammie flung the door open and grabbed Bill to hug him. She buried her head into his chest and began to sob.

"It isn't fair."

"I know…"

Bill held Sammie in his arms and brushed her hair with his hand.

"Every time one of them dies, it's so hard. It's like losing a member of your family. Claudia was hard but she was family, too. I just wish they didn't have to leave."

Bill spoke as softly and gently as he could.

"I know, but we all have to leave some time…"

"It's just…so…hard…"

Bill stood holding Sammie for a while longer until they heard the ambulance engine roaring up the hill.

"Come on. Let's go do what they need us to do."

"Okay."

The EMT and Paramedic pulled their equipment out of the back of the ambulance and headed inside to get Claudia. They gently placed her on the mattress of the gurney and strapped her down. When they filed by, the residents looked down at the floor and wept. They were seeing her so differently now compared to the night before when she had been so full of life and miraculous sounds.

Tilley came to Bill.

"Sheriff Tilley reportin', Sir. One down and out."

"I know, Tilley. Thanks"

Tilley looked at Bill for more orders and then just looked off into the distance with a glazed look in his eye when Bill didn't respond.

"One down and out..."

Sammie repeated Tilley's report.

"Yeah..."

Bill reached for her hand and gave it a squeeze.

Sammie turned and ran to the bathroom.

"I better go see if she's okay."

"Yes, Lucy, please do that."

While Lucy was tending to Sammie, Bill began to think about the residents again and how their lives had all turned out so differently than what they had probably expected. He wondered who would be next? Wilma? Tilley? Maybe even Sammie or himself! Death was no respecter of anyone, and the residents of Turkey Feather had already long been short on respect.

He went to the office to sit down for a while and be alone. As he looked out his window, he found himself pondering the meaning of life. Why things were the way they were. All the usual questions. Some of it made no sense to him and the justices of life made absolutely no sense whatsoever. The only thing Bill knew for certain was that his own life needed to make something of itself before he ended up in a place like Turkey Feather. Bill was terrified of that thought given what he had seen and experienced in just a short time already working with the old, the down, and the out.

Bill picked up Claudia's file from the very place he had flung it a few weeks previously. He glanced through it for any notes on what to do. There was a small sticky note tucked in the fold that had "attorney" written on it with a phone number. Bill had seen the note before, but it was folded up so tightly, he thought it was trash. He placed the note on the corner of his phone to call later. He had flipped through the file several times before but this time, he found another small envelope with a clasp on it tucked in between some papers written in German. It was a tiny, unusually shaped envelope. Bill opened it and found an old photo of a beautiful young girl in a dark dress. He assumed it must have been Claudia. He stared at the picture intently. It brought a tear to his eyes to think of how Claudia had been changed to her present state. Life was just so unfair. So unfair.

Bill picked up the phone to call the number he found in Claudia's file. After about a dozen rings, an elderly gentleman's voice with a thick German accent came on the line.

"'Hallo? Dis is Mistuh Richta. Who is dis?"

"Uh…Mister Richta, this is Bill Handley. I'm that administrator here at Turkey Feather Rehabilitation and Assisted Care Life Center. I'm calling about Claudia Saltzmann."

"Ah yes…Claudia. I've been expecting a call from someone regarding her affairs. How is dear Claudia?"

"Well, sir, she passed away this morning."

"Yes. I assumed she may have "passed away", as you say. Vat do you need me to do?"

"Well, Mr. Richta, I'm not exactly sure what I need. This is the first time I've run into anything like this and there isn't a lot of information to go on regarding Claudia's affairs."

"No, I suppose not. Ve took care of everyting for Claudia because of her delicate condeeshun. If you vant, I can send you everyting you will need. It is a relatively simple transahctshun. Give me a day or so and I vill have everyting taken care of for you and might I add my…uh…congratchulayshuns, if I may say so."

Bill was taken aback at Mr. Richta's statement.

"You mean condolences?"

"Uh…well…yah, condohlenses, too."

"Thank you. We're all upset over Claudia's passing. Thank you for your help. If you don't mind I'll get your contact information and place it in her file."

"Yes…yes…my name is Richta…spelled R-I-C-H-T-E-R. I lose a leetle in the translashun vat veeth mine ahkcent. Zee ahdress is 3710 Reek-tear Booleevahd, Suite A, Miahmee, Floreedah. You may deerect any other questions dere as vell"

"Thank you so much, Mr. Richter. I'll be in touch if I have anything."

"Yah. Tank you, too. I'm glad to be getting dees case feeneshed."

With that, Mr. Richter hung up. Bill thought the whole tone of the conversation was a little strange but with Claudia, nothing was surprising. Bill just chalked it up to another life lost in the passing of time. A life no one had much respect or care for and one that had flickered its last brilliant flame with the performance that had shut down Turkey Feather for one brief and beautiful moment.

Turkey Feather's Christmas dinner came and went without incident and some of the residents' families that visited regularly came by that evening. Christmas would be in two days, and everyone was still just as excited as the night of the big party. Things weren't quite the same without Claudia shaking it all up, but the excitement had built to a crescendo and nothing could stop the momentum of the season of seasons.

Bill hadn't had a lot of time to spend with the Quartet and they kept to themselves for the most part during the holidays. Dinner was coming to an end, and people were lingering in the dining room and hallway talking and fellowshipping with one another like Bill remembered his church would do for special events. Just as Bill was watching the guys over in a corner, Fred looked outside and went silent. He was watching something important and tracked whatever it was all the way to the front door. Fred stood up and stared at the door like he had seen a ghost. Lester waved the rest of the Quartet quiet.

Fred barely opened his mouth and whispered. "Baby…my baby…"

Standing there at the door was a woman in her early 40's with raven hair. She had a long wool coat on and a black sweater with acid-washed jeans and leather boots that laced up in front. The woman was Fred's daughter, Kaye Whiteowl. Tears ran down Fred's face as he shuffled toward her as fast as he could, his arms stretched out to embrace her.

"Baby! I can't believe you came! My Baby! It's been so long."

"I know, Pop. Too long." Fred grabbed her and held on as tightly as he could. Kaye laid her head on his shoulder and hugged him back. The scene caused the rest of the Quartet to look down at the floor and go silent. They may have been giving Fred his privacy, but Bill suspected it hurt them too bad to not be able to spend time with their own families. The scene was both moving and paralyzing at the same time. Most of the residents still hanging around the room stood and watched with a far-away look in their eye.

Fred must have caught himself in the moment because he stepped back and looked around and started to laugh.

"Hey everybody, this is my baby girl, Kaye. Come on and meet her!"

Poor Kaye. Fred's announcement brought residents from every corner of Turkey Feather. They thronged around her like a rock star. Kaye was smiling and laughing with Fred and trying to field handshakes as best she could, but they were coming in like the waves of yellow jackets disturbed from their duties. She was a good sport about it all and was kind to each of the greeters.

She and Fred finally got a moment to themselves. They sat in the corner of the dining room and held hands and laughed and cried and cried and laughed. Hilda brought them a cup of coffee on her way out and a biscuit.

Fred chided Hilda.

"Now, girl, you know I ain't supposed to have those."

"I know, Honey, but you got company and you cain't innertain without a little somethin' to eat or drink."

Fred smiled.

"Thank you. This is my daughter, Kaye. She came to see me for Christmas."

"I done heard. She's the talk of the town tonight."

Kaye smiled at Hilda and shook her head in agreement.

"You all take care and I'll see ya in the morning."

Kaye smiled again and Fred patted her on the hand.

"Thank you, girl."

Hilda left and Fred and Kay talked more. Finally, after a couple of hours, she hugged him and gathered her things to go.

"Kaye, I've missed you."

"I know, Pop. I've missed you, too. I really have."

"Why haven't ya come sooner? I love you so much."

"Pop...you just slipped away from us chasing your dreams. We all loved you, but you just had other things on your mind."

"I know...you're right...I'm so sorry, Baby. How is your Momma?"

"Momma is sick, Pop. She's bad off and has been for years."

"Oh, Kay...I'm so sorry. Please give her my...best...my...love..."

Fred began to cry.

"She knows Pop, but she couldn't keep living like we were. She had to raise us the best she could, and you were always working or chasing the dream with the rest of your friends, and we had to live."

"Yes. You're right, Kaye. I failed all of you. I gave up on you for my own selfish reasons. I never meant to hurt you, though. None of you. Especially not Rosie. Do you think I could see her some time? I would really love to see her one more time."

"Pop, I don't know, she's bad off like I said, and she can't get out much, but I'll try to see what I can do. I've got to go now, Pop. I'll try to get by more often, but I just needed to see you for a while this evening. I missed you and had to come."

"I'm glad you did, Baby. I've missed you so much and I love you so much."

"I love you, too, Pop. 'Bye now."

Kaye left and Fred sat back down at their table. He clasped his hands and watched her drive out of sight. Fred sat there for nearly thirty minutes after she was gone before he stirred again and went off to his room.

THE TURKEY FEATHER TRIO

CHAPTER FOUR

Before Bill left that evening, he sought out Lester to check on him and to see if there had been any more developments with their "project". He found Lester sitting in his room looking out the window. Bill hesitated before approaching then took a step forward. The floor let out a small creek and Lester turned his head.

"Hey, Bill. How's things?"

"Not bad. You?"

"Oh, just sittin' here contemplating."

"Contemplating what, my friend?"

Lester looked at Bill longingly and smiled a faraway smile. "I guess a lot of things. Life mostly. I sure didn't think it would turn out this way."

Lester wiped his nose to hide a tear running down his cheek.

Bill froze. He had never seen Lester like this, but he figured Fred's family visit may have precipitated a case of the blues for more than just Lester. He looked out the window again as if to say to Bill to leave him alone. He rested his hands on top of his cane and placed his chin over top of his hands. Lester began to cry harder, and the tears ran down the tip of his nose. Bill waited for Lester to cue him as to what to do or say but Lester never said a word. Whatever it was he was contemplating was his own. He wanted to keep it that way. Bill slipped out of the room and went home. That was the best thing he could have done for Lester at the time.

That night at home, Bill dreamt of Turkey Feather once again. He dreamt of the boys and their treasure hunt and all the others who might have come and gone before them. They had all shared something along life's journey. He dreamt of the girls and the way they took care of everyone, and he even dreamt of Hilda and her biscuits. It was the same dream every time, only, this time, all the players in Bill's mind were the same except for himself. This time he was actually a resident of Turkey Feather, and it was him who was being taken care of. Sammie and Tina were bringing him his meal and straightening his room and helping him out of the shower. Bill saw himself trying to leave and Sammie kept holding onto his arm trying to guide him back to a seat in the dining room like he had seen her do so many who were determined to try to leave the facility. Just when Sammie got him settled down, Tilley came in with a needle and equipment that looked like a weird set of headphones. Tilley had a wild look in his eye and kept repeating the same words over and over.

"How shocking to see you, how shocking to see you..."

Bill sat straight up in bed with his clothes soaked in cold sweat. Nothing like Tilley coming to give you a shock treatment to raise you up out of the bed in the middle of the night. Bill positioned himself on the edge of the bed and listened to the silence. He knew his dream was more than the stressors of the day at Turkey Feather. He was scared, too, like all the others. Bill didn't want to admit it to himself, but he had to. There was no other way of going about it but to face the fact that he, too, would be old one day. So would Sammie and Tina. Hilda and Frank were well on their way. Lucy was already there and didn't have much to show for all her years of hard work and life lessons. Bill guessed that was what he was most concerned about. Leaving a legacy, or a child, or something that would prove to the world that he had indeed been there and had lived a life worth living. Bill felt it was important to leave a piece of himself behind. He was afraid he would never figure out how to do that or spend an entire lifetime pursuing some dream that would never come true. Working a series of dead-end jobs, and paying bills, and driving old cars that needed more repairs than they were worth, and working on a house that never stopped needing attention, and then, at the end of it all, looking back over a lifetime and realizing it was just a way of living his life without living it was Bill's second worst fear. His first was doing it all alone.

A week later, Bill met with the Quartet to discuss their progress. He informed the group

that he had created a false profile for himself and had been asking around on the internet forums about the local history of the region. During one of his online discussions, the president of the Nickleville Historical Society opened a possibility. He mentioned a cannon that had supposedly been lost in the area during the Civil War. It seemed the cannon had been quite the local legend reaching celebrity status at some point. It was thought to be a rare brass cannon constructed for field artillery, but it might have been a Naval cannon stolen by the Union and being transported through enemy territory. There was even some speculation that it was the famous Whistling Dick and that it had been stolen by a rogue group of soldiers with links to the Knights of the Golden Circle. Either way, it was a clue to at least something and it might have been worth looking into. The meeting was adjourned when Sammie came to the office looking for everyone.

"What are you all up to?"

"Oh, don't you worry your pretty little head, Sweetheart!"

Raymond pinched her cheek as the boys filed out of the office one by one.

"What's up?" Sammie asked Bill.

"Not much. Just chatting with the fellas. You know how they like to talk."

"Hmmm…sounds like trouble to me…"

"Nah, just daydreaming mostly."

"This came for you in the mail. Addressed specifically to you. Must be important."

"Great! Thanks!"

Bill practically grabbed the package from Sammie's hands and tore it open.

"Wow…must be a love letter from your girlfriend…"

"Uh…no, not really…I'll tell you about it later."

"Oh. I see how you are. I know when I'M not wanted. I'll leave you alone to your package."

"Okay. Thanks."

Sammie was hurt and surprised at Bill's brisk reply, but she knew the package was something important for Bill to act that way.

Bill pulled the documents out of the package and began flipping quickly through them. He found a note from Mr. Richter. The note was short and only offered cursory directions written in chicken scratch. Bill tried to make something out of the words to no avail. He found a few pictures tucked neatly between the papers and then he found a document that looked to be a piece of financial information. What he saw next nearly blew his mind. It was something that not even Raymond or Mavis or anyone could have ever been able to come up with on their own. It seemed that Miss Claudia was not at all who or what she had appeared to be.

Claudia R. Saltzmann was a seventy-eight-year-old Jewish Holocaust survivor. She had been a daughter to one of Europe's most successful chocolatiers before World War II. The family empire had been destroyed by the Nazis but not before her father, who was a man of great vision, transferred most of his money to banks throughout the United States, particularly, Texas, where distant relatives lived. Claudia, however, was not as fortunate. She and her sister, Nina, were captured by Gestapo agents as they were leaving to meet the family on their escape voyage to America.

Claudia and Nina spent the next three months as prisoners of war and were labeled as enemies to the German motherland. Upon discovering their prized talent as confectioners, one of the Nazi Colonels had the Saltzmann sisters transferred to his charge. While there, the Colonel forced them to live like dogs in the storage room of the kitchen. The Colonel slapped Nina so hard once that her eyeball popped partially out of its socket. To avenge Nina, Claudia thrust a set of kitchen shears into the Colonel's thigh. The Colonel then had the guards hold Claudia down while he whipped her bare body and beat her from head to toe until she was unable to walk. Mercifully, he transferred Claudia and Nina to a death camp where Claudia lost most of her hearing due to her injuries. On their journey to the camp, the soldier in charge of their transfer sold the girls to a German aristocrat to use as his personal attendants.

During a raid on Nazi supporters, the girls were rescued by a battalion of Allied troops and sent to the United States to live with the distant relatives their father had been in contact with. Their mother and father had since died from the grief of leaving their daughters behind. Claudia had a nervous breakdown from the stress of her nightmares and was never able to maintain a life of her own. Nina, however, accessed her father's money and revived the family business by using the wealth she made with her chocolatier skills. Eventually, she invested heavily in the computer and oil industries. All told, at last count, Claudia R. Saltzman, demon-possessed or not, was worth well over nineteen million dollars. Bill fell back into his chair with his mouth hanging open.

It seems that Mr. Rounder was a customer friend of Nina's while they all lived in Texas. Their friendship was purely innocent and had lasted for years. Rounder served as sort of a big brother to Claudia during the time. He moved away to the peaceful solitude of Appalachia when he retired at the very young age of fifty-two. Rounder saw the need for a place like Turkey Feather and opened a whole string of other facilities along with it.

He and Nina only ever exchanged yearly Christmas cards until one day he got a call from Nina saying she was dying of cancer. Claudia would have no place to go. Knowing his business, Nina asked Rounder to take her in and make sure she was well-cared for. Rounder agreed but was surprised to see how badly Claudia had deteriorated upon her arrival. Nevertheless, he had made a promise to an old friend and did the best he could with Claudia. Of course, she would never want for anything, but her condition had left her unable to really know that. She was still a fighter and could curse like an angry, drunken sailor, but she would never be aware of what she was doing. When Nina passed away a short while later, Rounder created a trust in Claudia's name. Fortunately, he had also made all the necessary financial and power-of-attorney arrangements as well. On top of that, there was a deed made out in Claudia's name as sole owner of the buildings and real property that housed Turkey Feather Rehabilitation and Assisted Care Life Center. Apparently, Claudia was both princess and pauper of Turkey Feather, only, in this case, she was the lone queen. Along with the deed was another official looking document. Bill examined it closely. It was a notarized letter signed by Mr. Richter, Nina Saltzmann Rounder, and John Rounder.

"Nina Rounder?!" Bill whispered to himself. "What the...? Could she be? Yes, she would have to be. Claudia was Mr. Rounder's sister-in-law! I gotta talk to Richter about this."

Bill dialed Richter's office. The familiar accent came over the line. "Hallo? Dis is Richta. Who am I tahlking weet?"

"Mr. Richter, this is Bill Handley from Turkey Feather Rehabilitation and Assisted Care Life Center. I received your package. I need to speak with you for a minute."

"Yesss, Mista Hahndley. Vat can I do fohr you?"

"Well, I need some explanation about what this information means. Am I correct in reading that Claudia is worth nineteen million dollars?"

"Nineteen meelyan, sree hundred towsahnd ahnd some chainge to be exact.'

"What am I supposed to do with all this financial information you sent?"

"Vell, I tink you had betta get some finahnshul aseestance very soon. Ve can continue to help you, or you can find your own people to do ze job."

"What do you mean my own people?"

"Deed you read ze entire contents of ze package, Mr. Hahndley? In it, you vill find a note that eenstructs you on how to handle dis mahta. Zere ees a notariced letta signed by Mista and Meesus Rahnda grahnting the rights of ahdmeenahstrashun to whoevah vas to take on ze pozeeshun of ze bawss at ze faceeluhty upon ze time of Claudia's death. Zat vould be you and yohr staff, Mista Hahndley. Zat is why I spoke of congratchulayshuns een our preeveeus conversashun. I see dat you have no idea of vat I am speakeen of so I vill enlighten you a beet. As you know from ze infomayshun in ze dockumints, Claudia leeved a vahry hahsh life ven she vas yunga. Upon reunighting vith Neena, her life took a tuhn for zee bettah eef you vill. Neena vas beegeening hur beezness and vas becoming quite sooksesfool. Jahn Rahnda vas a dahshing yung petrohleum eenjuhnear vith deveelish good looks who hahd moved dere ahfta grajuateen kohlidge. He vas ahlrehdy feelthy reech from his vork in ze oil fields of Tahxus. The two fell in love at fuⁿst sight and vere soon mahrried. Mista Rahnda's mootha became gravely eel and he vent back home to Neekleveele to care for her. She hahd been placed een a nuhseen home dat vas fah, fah, soobstahnduhd. Mista Rahnda vatched his mootha die because of ze lack of kehreen staff membuhs and poleetical beeyahckrahcee and he vowed to make a change for uddahs. He began a streeng of ahseested kair seentahs to kair fah de eendahgent. He ahnd Neena trahveeled back ahnd fort between Neekleveele ahnd Tayxas fohr a few yeeahs but ze stress of mayntayneen Neena's sooksesfool beezness vore ze two down. Zeir love remained strong boot unfortyoonahtley zey vent zeir sehparaht vays. Neetha of dem evah mahrried ahgheen. Boath hahd extreemley genahrus hahts and ahgreed dat it vould be best for Claudia to stay een one of ze seentahs vere Jahn vould vatch hur. Eet vas ahslo deesided dat hur ahsets vould be deestribyuted to ze ahdmeenahstrashun at ze seentah vich she stayed een exchange foh ze exteenseeve kair and komfoot provided to Claudia frohm ze seentah stahff. Mista Rounda hahnd-peeked hees stahff at Tuhkey Fedda to eenshyor Claudia reseeved ze prahpa kair. He was pahteekulahly eemprehssed vith yoo, Mista Hahndley."

"Me? How could he be impressed with me? We only talked twice and once was over the phone."

"Mista Rahnda ees a very smaht man. He hahs eyes all ahround. Eet vould seem dat Miss Heelda is Mista Rahnda's cozen."

Bill ran his hand through his hair.

"Oh boy...didn't see that one coming. Good thing I've tried to tolerate her..," he thought.

"Eet vould seem dat Mista Rahnda is so eemprehssed vith yoo dat he vants you to take ovah hees eentiah line of kair homes. Dere are twenty-three of deem all toogethah. Ah yoo eentahrehsted, Mista Rahnda?"

"Do what? Are you kidding me? He wants me to take over his facilities? I had no idea he had that many. I...I don't know...that's a big responsibility. I don't know if I could do that right now. There's a lot going on that I'm trying to put together and I wouldn't want to miss anything."

"Truhst me, Mista Handley. You vill be able to come and go as you please. You vill be in chahge of yohr own skehdyul and you vill seemply be the ovahseeah makeen shua dat each seentah is ran corechtly. Eef you can do so fohr von of deem, you can do so fohr awl of deem."

"I don't know, Mr. Richter. I just don't know. There's so much here to do and there's he Quartet."

"Qwahtet? Vat is dees Qwahtet?"

"It's a group of the men here who have a project I'm helping them with. Sort of adventurers working on a history project."

"I see. Conseeder it, Mistah Hahndley. It comes veeth a very nice sahlary and beeneefeets pahckage."

"I don't know. I'll think about it and get back to you."

"Please do. Now, fohr ze rehst of ze infomayshun. Ze fuhnds of Mees Claudia vill now be placed into an ahcount to be used for ze ruhning of Tuhkey Fedda. Yoo ah soulvint, Mista Hahndley. Ze proveezhoons of ze ahgreemeent eevin eenclude ze coonstrookshun of a settlement on ze prahpuhtee dat yoo may leeve een for ze doorashun of yohr life. As I said before, Mista Rahnda and Neena ver kind-hahted people. You shood be so kind een retuhn."

"I understand. I understand completely. Thank you, Mr. Richter. How long do I have to let you know my decision?"

"You hahve oonteel you deeside. Eet ees compleeetly oop to you."

"Wow. I'll get back to you soon as possible. Thank you Mr. Richter."

"Tank you, Mista Hahndley. Good luhk to you. I vill fohrwahd enny udcah infomayshun you should need prahmplty."

"Alright. Thank you, again, Mr. Richter. Goodbye."

Bill was numb afterward and all he could do was shake his head in disbelief. So that was it. Claudia was worth millions and now she was gone and had never enjoyed one dime of it except for the simple comforts given her by the staff at Turkey Feather. What a story. What an unbelievable story. The girls would never believe this one. Not even "Hollywood" could come up with something as far-fetched as this. Bill closed the file and put it on top of the others. He took a minute to reminisce on Claudia's behalf. It was simply too unbelievable to fathom. The fact that she had survived all these years after the atrocities she suffered was miracle enough let alone her financial situation. Bill just sat there in amazement. It came to him that he was going to have to tell the girls about it all at some point. This was a delicate situation that had to be handled just as delicately. Bill had no intention of changing anything until he was sure it was okay to proceed with any plans that may arise from Turkey Feather's new fortune. He knew the girls had great hearts, but he had to be careful.

When Bill went in to look for everyone, Hilda met him at the door.

"Hi, Boss!"

"Hi, Hilda."

Bill was overwhelmed with emotion, and he grabbed Hilda to give her a hug.

"Uh…Boss…what was that for?"

"Just for being you, Hilda. Just for being you."

"Gorsh. Thanky."

"Hilda, why didn't you ever tell anyone you were Mr. Rounder's cousin?"

"How'd you find that out?"

"Let's say a little birdie told me."

"Well, Boss…I guess I jus' didn't want folks thinkin' I was like my boy, Clovis. You know he's slow and all and I didn't want folks a-thinkin I was like him and couldn't find me a job on my own. I even applied for the

83

job here and used my middle name so's no one would know. Mr. Davies never suspected a thing, and I don't think Cousin John woulda cared one way or anuther cause he had offered me jobs before but I just wanted to do it on my own. Guess I'm kinda prideful. Cousin John shore likes you. He told me back over the summer that he thought you'd do good by this ol' place. I told him you was a good'un. Not like Davies."

"I appreciate that, Hilda. I really do. Your Cousin John is a special person, too."

"Yeah. He's purty good. He was always good to my Momma and me. He sent Clovis off to a school to learn how to weld without me even askin'. He liked Clovis even when he was little. He was always sendin' him cards fer his birfday with some money in 'em. Clovis done some work for him cleanin' up and all. They jest liked one another, I guess."

Hilda gathered her apron in her hands while she talked to Bill. She twirled and tugged at the knot of her apron string and never looked up once. Bill had no idea that Hilda's son was a slow learner. It seems Mr. Rounder's kindness knew no bounds.

"Hilda, can you get the other girls and meet me in the dining room as soon as you can?"

"Sure thang, Boss. Somethin' wrong?"

"No, Hilda. Not wrong at all. Not wrong at all…"

Bill smiled as he went back to the office to gather Claudia's paperwork. He knew how hard it was for him to believe so he wanted the proof to show everyone. He couldn't wait to see the looks on their faces and the reactions. Bill was like a kid again waiting to show his mother his grade card filled with all "A's".

Just about the time he stepped out of the office on his way back in, Lester showed up with a sense of urgency.

"Bill…come quick…It's Mavis. He fell through a hole in the ground big enough to swallow a car. He's down in there yelling in pain."

"Jesus Christ! What have you all been doing?"

"No time for that, Bill. You've got to come and help us."

"I'll call emergency services."

"NOOO!!! NO! You CAN'T! We found it. We found the lost cannon!"

"The what?!?!"

"The lost cannon! We found it. We took your information and started investigating and poking around here and there and found the cannon!"

Lester was short of breath.

"How the Devil did you find…never mind. We've got to get to Mavis! Where is he?"

Bill understood the urgency of having a senior citizen go missing but he was completely flustered to know that one of his keeps was down in a ditch God only knew where. He just hoped there were no broken bones or serious injuries and with Mavis you could never tell because of how much he put on.

"He's this way. Follow me."

Just as they were ready to turn the corner of the main building, Tilley popped up in Bill's face. Surprisingly, Bill had the wherewithal to speak to Tilley calmly.

"Tilley…go inside and tell the girls I said the meeting is cancelled. They're in there waiting on me but something's come up. Just tell them I'll talk to them later."

"Yes, sir! Sheriff Tilley is on the job!"

The urgency in Lester's voice grew more serious.

"Let's GO!"

Bill knew it was a real emergency and that Mavis could be in serious trouble. They moved as fast as Lester could and kept going until they came to the edge of the woods. Lester led Bill down a narrow path to the edge of a small slope. Fred and Raymond were standing at the side of what looked to be a sink hole. Together, Bill and Lester gingerly made their way down the slope helping one another as they went along sliding and side-stepping down to the others.

When he got to him, Bill saw that Fred was as white as a sheet and Raymond's teeth were chattering. Bill feared they had both gone into shock.

"Okay, boys. What happened?"

"We were comin' down the side of the hill and Mavis climbed up on this log and when he slid his other leg over, the log and Mavis both just busted through the ground."

Fred was shaking and had a weeping sound in his voice.

Raymond took over the story at that point.

"He yelled as he went down and then we heard a sound like somebody tryin' to ring a bell all dull-like. We come over to the hole and looked down and saw him. He was wigglin around but now he's just a-layin' there."

Bill looked down into the hole. Luckily, it was only about four feet deep, and the log was sticking up partially out of the hole. It would be easy enough to get to Mavis and Bill managed to maneuver himself down next to him.

"I'll be damned..." he whispered.

"Yeah, me too."

Mavis spoke to Bill and looked at him pitifully. Bill could see the pain in Mavis' eyes.

Bill placed his hand on Mavis' shoulder.

"It's going to be okay, Mavis. Don't worry."

"I ain't too worried yet..."

"Good. We'll get you up out of there as quick as we can get the emergency responders here."

"What about our cannon? They'll know."

"It's time the whole world knows. Don't worry about that, either."

With that, Bill shot a glare at the other three and they quietly understood they had better not protest. This was it. The end of their quest. Their glorious moment they had worked their entire lives for and one of them had almost lost their life over it. Bill was filled with both relief and sadness because he knew the find meant so much to the boys. He just didn't know what else to do at this point. When the responders got there, word would spread like wildfire and the whole world would descend upon Turkey Feather.

Bill had to come up with a plan and quick. He sent Raymond to tell Sammie to call emergency services. He gave him instructions on exactly what to tell her. Nothing more than a small accident at this point. She, nor the responders, needed to know more than that. It would only complicate things even more. In the meantime, he began looking at Mavis' predicament and tried to see how bad he was lodged in the hole. From what he could tell, the cannon had dislodged and rolled against Mavis when he broke through the surface and had him penned against the ground at the bottom. For such an important piece of history, the canon had been carelessly buried to say the least and Bill figured that the group of soldiers who had presumably stashed it there had full intentions of retrieving it.

"Mavis, you've got to listen to me carefully. Try to move your arms and legs a little and see if they hurt you at all."

Mavis squirmed.

"I can move everything pretty good, but my right arm is stuck under me."

"That's good. You might have bruised it or, at most, broken it but we can fix that later."

Bill motioned for Lester to come to him.

"Okay, Les, this is what we're going to do. I saw a log with a narrow fork in it when I was coming down the hill. It looked sturdy, and I think we can use it to possibly get Mavis loose. You and Fred bring me the log and I'll pry the cannon up enough for you two to reach in and pull Mavis the best you can."

"I don't know, Bill, what if…"

Bill snapped at Lester.

"Look! You guys dragged me into this now do what I say unless you want the credit for finding that cannon going to someone else."

"Right!"

Lester hurried off with Fred to fetch the log. Fred was having trouble carrying his end, but they managed to make it back.

"Here it is, Bill. Is this the one?"

"Yes, good job. Now help me position it into place."

The three of them placed the log into the hole next to Mavis.

"We might press the log against you a little Mavis and if we hurt you, just let us know."

"Oh, no problem there. I'll yell right good."

Bill could tell Mavis was becoming both anxious and excited at the thought of being freed from his earthen prison.

"Hang tight, Mavis. I think this will work."

With the log in place, Bill moved the end back and forth enough to get a solid fit. Then he pried the cannon upwards with as much strength as he could muster.

"Get in there! Pull him out!"

Lester and Fred reached in and grabbed Mavis by the shirt sleeve and tugged at him as hard as they could. Mavis tried to help by kicking his feet and pushing himself out while being pulled through the dirt and rocks.

"Is he clear?!?!"

"Yeah, Bill! He's clear!"

Bill couldn't hold the cannon up anymore and let it drop back down. It dislodged even more and mad a dull thud when it landed. It narrowly missed Mavis' foot and rested in the indention it made in the ground.

"Dear God…that was a Helluva thing."

Bill looked at Mavis and rolled his eyes. He thought about giving the three of them a scolding, but he knew the emergency services crew would be arriving any minute.

"Let's just get away from this cannon right now. I'll help Mavis up the hill and you two cover it with some sticks and leaves as best you can. Come on, Mavis"

Bill put Mavis' arm around his neck and the two of them started up the incline. Lester and Fred stood and watched as they ascended.

Bill turned and looked at Lester.

"You better hurry up with that thing."

Lester gave him a solemn stare.

"Thank you. You don't know what this means to us."

"Yeah. Apparently, I don't. I'm just glad it's over. We'll figure out what to do later."

"Okay."

Just as Bill and Mavis topped up to the lawn, Sammie came rushing over with a two-member crew of emergency service members.

"We'll take him from here."

Sammie looked at Bill worried.

"What happened?"

"Oh, the boys were walking around in the woods taking a hike and Mavis slipped and slid down the hillside. They panicked and came to get me. I think he's okay, but he might be banged up a little."

"That bunch has got to stop this stuff. One of them is gonna get hurt bad."

"That's what I told them."

"Where are Lester and Fred."

"They'll be along soon. They were collecting leaves or something."

"You left them?"

"They're fine. I told them to be careful."

"Good LORD."

Bill hated to lie to Sammie, but he had made a promise and a pledge to the boys that he would help them as best he could. The incident was over no matter how serious it could have been and now they had to figure out what to do with the cannon and getting it squared away. Bill realized what it meant to them to get the credit for the find but he didn't know how to go about facilitating that right now. The wheels were turning as Bill was sure they were with the boys, and he figured that they would need to have a pow-wow soon to discuss the recent development. It was hard to determine how much that thing weighed, and God only knew what it would take for the five of them to get it to sunlight.

The next morning, Bill came into Turkey Feather and asked where Lester was. Sammie pointed upstairs and never looked up from folding laundry. When Bill found Lester, he was sitting on the side of his bed alone in the room.

"Hey, Mister. How are ya?"

"I suppose as well as can be expected. Heard anything from Mavis?"

"Not yet, Les. I'll check on him in a few minutes. Listen, what happened yesterday…"

"I know, Bill. It was a fool thing to do. I've been thinking a lot about the spot we've put you in. I'm sorry. I know you must be upset with all of us but we're so close. We're almost there. If we can just decipher that poem, we'll have everything."

"Are you serious, Lester? The poem?! It was just a ruse made up by some war-time Captain with Post-Traumatic Stress Disorder! Mavis almost got killed, Lester. It WILL stop NOW! I know you've spent a lifetime looking for this cannon. You've found it so let's share it with the world and let folks come and inspect it and make a big fuss over it while you and the boys sit and hold court. Answer some questions, maybe do some morning shows and a few interviews, and be done with it. It has got to come to an end sometime and that time is now."

"Bill – don't you see? The cannon was only the beginning of what is hidden around here somewhere. If Captain Fink had the cannon itself buried in a makeshift pit, that gold is somewhere nearby."

"I won't hear of it again, Lester. The answer is an emphatic NO!"

"Bill – be reasonable. You want to find the gold as badly as we do. It's in your soul now and you're part of us. We've all got to continue with the hunt. It's here! I know it is. That cockamamie tapestry means something else why would a war Captain waste his time working on something that was considered woman's work back then."

Bill stood there looking at Lester. He couldn't believe what he was hearing. Lester was determined to die looking for this treasure. Lester's eyes glistened like a child's waiting for Christmas and Bill just shook his head.

"Lester, what's it going to take? How far will you go?"

"I'll go to my grave if that's what it takes and so will the others. It's all we have left. That treasure and each other. We'll lose the cannon to a museum somewhere, but that gold is ours!"

"Lester...I just can't."

"FINE!"

Lester was furious.

"Be that way! We'll all show you! We already did once, and we will again! Just go on and leave us be."

Bill was shocked at Lester's outburst, but he couldn't keep feeding into the delusion that there was gold on the property to be found by a bunch of old codgers. If Bill had to transfer them away from Turkey Feather, he would be forced to do so for their safety.

"Lester, let me warn you. If you and the boys keep this up, I'll be forced to move all of you to other facilities. It's a matter of safety at this point."

"YOU WOULDN'T!"

"Yes, Lester, I would. I can't have one of you dying because of a treasure hunt."

"You'll be sorry if you do that Billy Boy. You'll be sorry. Remember, we have nothing left to lose."

"Is that a threat, Lester?"

"It's whatever you want it to be. Now just leave me alone and get out of here!"

Lester turned away from Bill and mumbled under his breath.

"I'll show him and all of them..."

P. RAY LEWIS

CHAPTER FIVE

Bill left the room and went to the office. He was heartbroken and disgusted with Lester. He picked up the file he kept on the boys and their search and slung it across the room. When the papers settled, the journal was lying on the couch open to the poem. Bill read it over and over. He didn't want to read it, but the search had taken him in. He was so torn over stopping the boys and letting them search. Part of him thought there was no harm, but the other part thought if the pursuit continued someone would get hurt extremely bad or even killed. There were enough cliffs and caves and abandoned mines in the area to swallow someone up to never be heard from again.

Bill looked out the side door of the office across the front lawn. It was a beautiful rolling lawn with various bushes dotting the landscape. He had never noticed before the huge weeping willow tree with its branches and long switches of leaves hanging down. There were so many of them. The limbs of the tree knotted and swirled upward and outward like giant arms pointing to something they couldn't quite reach. Funny that Bill had never noticed that particular tree. Most of the trees were hardwoods and pines off in the woods but the oaks were the predominate tree on the estate. Bill figured some bird had maybe dropped a seed in a hole and it had just taken root by chance. He looked back toward the journal, and something stopped him. He read the journal all the way through again stopping at the part about the tapestry and its cryptic message. Could the tree be part of it? It was a long shot, but Bill was going to consult with the boys about his theory. He went into the house and flew up the stairs. Lester was nowhere to be found.

Tina was straightening the upstairs room.

"Where's Lester?"

"He left out of here about ten minutes ago. Dropped down over the back of the property. Said he was goin' for a visit."

Bill felt a sickening welling up in his stomach.

"Did he say where he was going?"

"Never mentioned where he was goin'. Just that he was gonna go for a visit. What's the problem? Him and the rest of the guys go on visits all the time."

"Yeah, but the problem this time is he has no one to visit."

Tina gave Bill a quizzical look.

"Have you seen any of the rest of the gang?"

"Not since this mornin'. They were all in the dining room talking after breakfast. They seemed in pretty good spirits then."

"Okay. Thanks"

The uneasy feeling in the pit of Bill's stomach was growing. Surely one of the guys would know something about where Lester had gone off to.

Bill poked his head into the dining room and saw Fred and Raymond sitting in the corner jabbering away like two schoolboys.

"Guys – have you seen Lester?"

Fred raised his eyebrows.

"If you're lookin fer that ol' fart, he left outta here in a huff earlier. Said he was goin off to where no one knowed where he would be."

"Well, I suppose that huff was my part. He and I had some words over the 'you-know-what' and I'm afraid he's exceedingly mad."

Raymond spoke up and laughed at Bill.

"Don't pay attention to that ol' cuss. He'll be back when his pout wears off. He always does."

"I hope you're right."

94

Bill trailed off his sentence with a concerned stare and left the dining room. He walked around Turkey Feather wringing his hands and wondering what could be of Lester. Deep down, Bill knew there was something wrong this time and that Lester may have gone and done something foolish. Sammie flagged Bill from the door attached to the back of the kitchen.

"Bill! Come quick!"

Bill ran to Sammie and asked what the matter was. "Have you seen Lester?"

"No. I've been looking for him most of the morning. He and I had some words earlier and I can't find him anywhere."

"Well...one of the cab drivers who usually picks him up just called and said Lester had him drop him off at the train depot over at Queen Station. Said he watched him buy a ticket for somewhere. Didn't see where but said Lester was acting funny and mumbling something under his breath."

"Oh, dear Jesus...he's trying to run away. I threatened to transfer him and the others this morning if they didn't quit this cannon and treasure business and he blew up."

"Uh...Bill...what are you talkin' about cannons and treasure?"

Bill almost threw up. He hadn't meant to slip up like that and now Sammie would be curious as a cat to find out what was going on. Bill thought the world of Sammie, but she could be tenacious when she thought something was afoot.

'Oh...I don't know...just some nonsense that Lester talks about sometimes. I'll tell you about it later. Right now, I've got to get to Queen Station and find out where Lester is going."

"Do you know where you're goin'?"

"Dammit! No! I have no idea where it is."

"Get in and I'll drive you. You seem to be pretty upset yourself right now. Let me drive and you just relax and gather your thoughts. Isn't that what you tell me to do all the time?"

"Yes, but you can't say anything..."

"I'm not going to say anything about the treasure, there Blackbeard. Let's just find Lester right now and go from there."

Bill appreciated Sammie's understanding. They hurried to her car and left Turkey Feather in a cloud of dust. Sammie remained quiet while Bill's mind raced with tragedies upon tragedies that could have befallen Lester. He had only been gone a few hours, but that man could get into all kinds of trouble in that amount of time.

When they arrived at Queen Station, the ticket agent was closing for lunch.

Bill cried out to him from across the terminal.

"Wait!"

The gentleman gave Bill a stern look.

"Whaddaya want? I got a hot date with a pastrami and rye in about 30 seconds."

"We're looking for someone."

"Ain't we all, Buddy, ain't we all?" the ticket agent replied dryly.

"No. This is serious. His name is Lester McManamay. He's a resident at Turkey Feather Rehabilitation and Assisted Care Life Center. He's missing. Well, he's not exactly missing but we think he's running away."

"Look, pal. It don't make any difference to me what he's doin' or where he's from. I can't give you any information on anybody except this. An old guy came through here a few hours ago and took the 10:37am train out west. That's all I can say. If you got problems bigger than that, call one of them Silver Alerts and let the whole world know your friend is missin' or ran away."

"Look. He and I got into a fight this morning and he left in a huff. He's mad and not thinking straight. Please. Help us find him."

"Sorry, buddy. That's all the information I can give you. Rules say I probably gave you too much already."

The ticket agent slammed the window door shut.

Bill ran his fingers through his hair. He and Sammie went back to her car. On the way back, Bill racked his brain for somewhere that Bill might have run off to. He had no friends or family that anyone knew of and with Lester, he could be heading anywhere. Bill looked out the window and worried as much as he could.

Back at Turkey Feather, Bill and Sammie got Tina to help them ransack Lester's things. Lester was so mad he didn't even take any clothes with him. Apparently, he had left with just the clothes on his back. Nothing. Not a clue as to where he might have gone. They went through everything which was about three drawers of worn-out socks and underwear, his Turkey Feather clothes, and a few old pictures of him and the boys that he had kept from down through the years.

"Hey – where did these pictures come from? Isn't that Fred and Raymond with Lester? There's Mavis, too. By the way, Bill, Mavis is on his way back from the hospital. He checked out okay."

Mavis! If anyone would know where Bill would be going, Mavis would.

Bill sat in the office waiting on Mavis and leapt to his feet when the ambulance transport brought him in.

"Mavis, I have to talk to you!"

"Gorsh, Bill, I knowed you missed me but I'm right here. Calm down!"

"I can't find Lester."

"Oh, he probably took a cab somewhere or he's on a walk around here some place."

"No. This is different. He did take a cab, but he took it to the train station. I called the cab company and the driver saw him buy a ticket, but he didn't know where. Lester just mumbled during the whole ride there and never spoke to him. Les and I had some words this morning and he took out of here when I was doing some paperwork."

"Well, he ain't never bought no train ticket before. I don't know what that's all about."

"We have to find him."

"Yeah, sounds serious. Lester is a funny feller sometimes. If he gets really perturbed, he'll fly off the handle and do some fool thing most times."

"Has he ever mentioned going off somewhere?"

"Well, no, not that I recall. He said somethin' about goin' off somewhere years ago when he retired but he retired here. It wouldn't have been my first choice but I'm here, too, so what do I know? You don't never know with Lester. He keeps a lot bottled up and don't tell nobody much about what he's thinkin'."

"Try to remember anything at all. I'm afraid he might go too far and not be able to get back. I have some information I think will set us on course to the real treasure."

"Treasure? I thought the cannon was the treasure!"

"It's just part of it, Mavis. The best is yet to come."

With that, Bill began to rush off to look for clues as to where Lester might have gone.

Mavis shouted at Bill as he escaped the conversation.

"Can't ya tell the rest of us?!"

Bill heard Mavis in the distance and purposely ignored him. He was on a greater mission right now and the main goal was to find Lester. He went over to the office. Bill called the authorities to have Lester put on a Silver Alert. Even though he hadn't been gone 24 hours, Bill wanted to make sure as many people as possible were aware of Lester's absence. He called the Sheriff as well and the emergency services for the surrounding counties just to cover his bases. When he had done as much as he thought possible, Bill left for his house. Just as he got to his car, he saw Sammie walking toward him. Maybe she had some information.

"Sammie! Heard anything on Lester yet?" Bill yelled out to her.

"Nothin' yet. What have you all been up to? What's up? What caused all this with Lester? Why the panic?"

"You wouldn't believe me if I told you."

"Try me. Not much surprises me and obviously it's important for Lester to leave and for you to be in such a tizzy so spill the beans."

"Sammie, I just can't. It's something that means a lot to the boys, and I just can't wreck it for them."

"Well, considering you have a national manhunt on for Lester, I think all of us deserve to know."

Bill knew Sammie was right, but he couldn't break the trust the boys had put in him. He just looked at her with intense eyes and got in the car. Before he pulled out, he stopped to look at Sammie again.

"I'm sorry. I hope you understand."

Sammie shrugged her shoulders and cocked her head to the side while turning away from Bill. Bill could feel her heart hardening toward him. Sammie would just have to trust Bill on this one. He hated to be so secretive but there were some things a man just had to keep to himself, and this was one of those times.

When Bill came in through the door, the phone was ringing.

"Hello?"
"Hey, Chief? This is Hilda. Hey, I think I might know where Lester might have gone."

Great…that was all Bill needed then. An amateur sleuth at her finest.

"Where might that be, Hilda?"

"Well, he might have gone off all the way to California. My cousin, Steve, who works maintenance for the railroad and sometimes he works for the fire department when he's off from the railroad but he don't work for the railroad every day cause he's on for a day and then off for two or three days…"

"Hilda, please, tell me where you might think Lester might be!"

"Oh, right Chief, sometimes I get carried away with talkin' too much and I start tellin' all about ever'thing…"

"HILDA! WHERE IS LESTER?"

"Sheesh, sorry, Chief. I think he might have gone off to California! Cousin Steve told me him and some of the fellas from the railroad was talkin' to the man at the train depot at Queens and he told 'em about some old man who come in and bought his self a ticket all the way to California. Didn't say where, though, but he keeps a big map with little pins on it where people buy tickets to, and he put one of them little pins in the map when he sells a ticket. Cousin Steve said it looked like the pin was over next to the edge on the coast."

"Califronia? Why on earth would he go to Califor…?"

Then it dawned on him. Bill remembered seeing the newspaper

photograph about the search for the cannon and reading the caption where Lester said he and the boys might retire to San Diego. He hated to think that Hilda might be right, but it was worth a shot. San Diego being a coastal town it sounded like she might know what she was talking about this time.

"Thanks, Hilda! I'll check it out."

"Okay, Chief. If you need me to do anything, I got family out west and they know all kinds of people and they can check it out for us."

"Hilda, I'll talk to you in the morning. Thanks."

Bill hung up the phone while Hilda yammered more about family and California and helping, and Bill just couldn't really listen to it anymore. If Hilda was right, Lester could very well have flown into enough of a rage to have bought a ticket to California. Lester was unusually upset over this whole thing which led Bill to think there was more going on than met the eye. Lester was out of his element since he and the boys had literally stumbled onto their find and Bill was worried that he couldn't handle the pressure of their semi-success.

Bill called the authorities and alerted them to the new developments. The sheriff said he would call the San Diego Police Department to look for a man fitting Lester's description. San Diego was a big place but surely Lester would stand out enough for someone to think it odd that a man of his age with no luggage would be roaming around out there like a lost puppy. Then again, it was San Diego, so all bets were off on Lester standing out. How in the world would Lester survive out there? Bill's mind raced with thoughts of awful things happening to Lester. He imagined everything from Lester getting locked away in an asylum to being beaten up and killed or thrown off a beach cliff.

That was it. A beach cliff.

Bill knew what Lester was up to now and where he was going. He recalled a conversation they had once about Lester wanting to go to California to see the ocean again and how Lester reminisced about the trip he had taken there with his wife when they were young. He remarked how it was the happiest trip of his life and how he wanted to go back there some day. Lester talked about the beautiful sunsets and how excited his wife was when she watched the dolphins playing in the surf. Bill remembered how Lester had teared up during the conversation and then just turned away to avoid talking about it anymore. Bill was certain that was where Lester was heading, and he thought he knew why, too.

Bill knew he had to go get Lester and he made the decision to tell Sammie what was going on. If he was going to retrieve the old codger, someone had to keep a watch on the boys' prize that they would trust. As much Hell as he gave Sammie, they adored her, and she babied them like they were all her own father. It would be a difficult trip but no more difficult than Lester's trip by train. All in all, it was just another adventure that Lester would be leading Bill on so he knew he would have to prepare accordingly. He checked Lester's file and rifled through his financial records. It seems that Lester could have afforded such a trip and even had a little fur while he was away. Apparently, all those trips he and the boys took treasure hunting had been strictly business. Lester hadn't really checked out much money to speak of until he left. Bill found a stack of bank account statements that showed Lester had nearly eight thousand dollars amassed over several years. The money was in several different local banks and Bill pretty much surmised that Lester was avoiding any suspicions over his personal worth by keeping the amounts in the accounts smaller so the T-men as he and the boys referred to them wouldn't get wise to what Lester was worth. Bill checked through some more of Lester's things and found a picture of him and his wife at Ocean Beach. Lester must have kept it all these years and since he found it on the top of the heap, Bill was positive he had gone there to see it one more time.

Now that he knew what he had to do about making the arrangements for a trip, it was time to sit Sammie down and tell her all about the treasure and the lifelong hunt for the cannon. Bill went to the dining hall of Turkey Feather with a mind full of swirling scenarios. Sammie was sitting in her favorite chair as if she was waiting for an explanation. Bill looked into her eyes and opened his mouth to speak when Sammie stopped him.

"How dare you come in here to speak to me, Bill Handley, when you've been hidin' somethin' from me all this time. Those guys are like my second fathers, and I've babied them for years. You come in here like you own the place and start talkin' to them and sneakin' around this place with them and now you're the big man on campus and they all run to you with everything under the sun and now one of them has gotten hurt and one is missin'. Who do you think you are?"

Bill had never seen Sammie with this much fire in her eyes and he knew she was right. He knew he had let things go too far and now they were in danger.

He also knew it was his fault, too.

"Sammie, I'm sorry…"

"Jack skippy you're sorry! You should have told me what was going on a long time ago because none of this would have happened to them. I would have put my foot down and put you in your place, but NOOO – I had to let you run in here and steal my heart and put my faith in you and trust in you and now you've gone and turned into a bigger fool than all of them put together!"

"Uh…I don't know what to say, Sammie…"

"Well, you better think of somethin' fast because we gotta go get Lester wherever he is. I hope to God you've figured out in that big brain of yours where he's at!"

"Well…yeah, I have a pretty good idea where he is."

"Then let's go get him!"

"It's not that easy, Sammie. It's kind of complicated."

"Complicated my hind end – get your junk and let's go. He can't have gone that far."

"That's just it, Sammie. He's in California."

"DO what?! California?!?!!"

"I think Lester is on his way to California."

"You think he's in California?"

"On his way to be exact."

"Why, I oughta knock the livin' crap outta you…"

With that, Sammie took a step toward Bill and tried to rush him. Bill reached out and put his hands on her shoulders to stop her from advancing but she slipped through his hands and punched him in the chest. While it didn't hurt Bill much, it took him by surprise.

"Do you realize what could happen to that old man in California? He could get killed! He'll be roamin' around out there like a homeless person and get picked up by the cops!"

"I know, Sammie. Just calm down. I'm going out there to get him."

"You're going out there to get him? We're going out there to get him! You've made a big enough mess of all of this already! I'm not about to let you screw it up anymore!"

"SAMMIE! LISTEN TO ME!"

Sammie blinked and stared at Bill wide-eyed not knowing what else to say. Apparently, she had said enough to get Bill riled enough to raise his voice at her, so she sat there and waited for him to finish whatever it was he had to say.

"Sammie, you've GOT to listen to me. This is going to sound crazy, but you need to know what's going on around here with the boys. Brace yourself because it's a wild ride.:

Bill sighed and Sammie still sat there looking at him and waited for him to continue.

"Okay…where to begin…First, let me apologize for keeping you in the dark. I promised the boys I wouldn't tell anyone because they swore me to secrecy, and I've tried to keep my word to them as best I could. I realize now that was probably not in their best interests considering what all has happened in the last several hours, but I gave them my word and I tried to keep it. Now, to say this is easy to tell you would be a lie but I'm going to try to make it as easy to understand as possible."

"Go ahead, smart guy. I'm not stupid."

"No one said you were stupid, Sammie, just listen."

Sammie shot darts at him through her eyes but motioned for him to go on with the story.

"First of all, this is something the boys have worked on for a long time. Apparently, they have worked on it for most of their lives and it's just now coming to be for them. I didn't want to spoil it because I thought it was innocent fun at first."

"What did you think was fun at first?"

"Their treasure hunting."

"Oh, that. You don't' really believe them with all of that, do you?"

"You know about it?!"

"I know they've been millin' around here since I've been here lookin' for God knows what. What do you know about it?"

"Plenty. They were telling the truth about the treasure. The only thing is that it wasn't exactly a treasure."

'Well then what was it?"

"It was a cannon. A big brass cannon and it's worth tens of thousands of dollars. Maybe hundreds of thousands to someone. Either way, it's a very important find and the boys are scared to death someone is going to steal it from them."

"Bill Handley, are you messin' with me?"

"Not one bit. They literally fell on top of it just over the hill. That's how Mavis got hurt. He fell into a pit that was covered with a bunch of old branches and leaves. It had been there almost a hundred years so a lot of stuff had grown over on top of it and anyone walking by would have never suspected a thing. Mavis just happened to be the lucky one to fall on top of it all."

"Where is it now?"

"It's still there. The boys and I covered it up as best we could and took Mavis out of there as quietly as possible. They will definitely want to go back for it so I'm going to have to come up with a plan for lifting a seven-hundred-pound cannon ten feet out of a hole big enough to lose a car in and located on an incline covered with slippery moss and leaves. That's going to be a picnic, I'm sure."

"How in the world is that gonna work?!"

"I don't know. I'll cross that bridge when I get to it. That's not the best of it. I think there's more to the cannon than meets the eye. I think there's gold stashed away somewhere around Turkey Feather, too."

"Do what? Now, Bill you're just pullin' my leg now.'"

"No, I'm not. I believe it's gold. I don't know if it's a cache of gold bars or coins, but I think it's here. When the boys first approached me to join the little charade, I did some research on the area and its history in relation to the Civil War. It seems this area was a real popular route for travelers and the Union Army used the cut through the mountains to head off the Confederate supply lines. There was a certain Captain Tiberius Fink who lived in the area that was rumored to have stolen the gold and hid it. It might even be hidden right here at Turkey Feather, but no one knows for sure. The boys even have a small tapestry they found, and a journal written by Captain Fink's wife. As crazy as it is, it all seems to be legitimate, but we haven't had time to fetter it all out. The boys have been searching on their own and I thought it was only right to let them keep looking since they'd been with it for so long already."

"Oh, dear GOD! Why didn't you tell me about this earlier? It's a thousand wonders ALL of you hadn't been killed lookin' for some crazy pot of gold at the end of the rainbow!"

"I know, Sammie. I know. I made a huge mistake by not telling you. I just thought it wasn't a big deal to be honest. I thought the boys would never find anything. Then, when they did…well, I just don't know what to do now."

"Geez, Bill. You've put us all in a heck of a mess, you know?"

"That's not all. Claudia left nineteen million dollars to Turkey Feather when she died, and she was Mr. Rounder's sister-in-law."

"Okay, now you ARE joking with me and pullin' my leg…right…? Bill, tell me you're joking."

"I couldn't make this stuff up. It's a long story like the one the boys have. Looks like Turkey Feather is just chock full of surprises. Sammie, I'll tell you more but right now I've got to go get Lester. I'm afraid he'll get hurt and you know how I feel about him. I can't let that happen to him."

"We all feel that way."

Sammie sat up in her seat and Bill turned to look over his left shoulder. Tina had been standing behind him and listening the whole time.

"Sorry. I didn't mean to eavesdrop, but I was cleanin' in the other room and heard almost everything. I'm so sorry. Please don't think I was snoopin' but what you said about Bill goin' to California…I think you're right. Before you came, Bill, sometimes he would sit and look at magazines that had pictures of beaches and just stare at them for hours. I tried to talk to him about beaches a few times, but he would just sit there and smile at me and change the subject."

Bill and Sammie looked at one another and they both knew that Tina should come with them. If anyone besides Sammie and Bill loved the place and its people, Tina did.

"I don't think you were snooping, Tina. I know you care about the boys as much as we do. How much did you hear?"

"Well, I know that Lester was pretty upset when he left, and I know that he went off somewhere. Probably California it seems. I didn't hear much other than that because I was runnin' back and forth doin' laundry."

"Oh no, I'm so sorry, Tina. I got so mad at Bill I completely forgot about helping'you."

"It's okay, Sammie. Honest. I know this is an important thing else Lester wouldn't have left his home."

At the mention of Lester's home, the three of them looked at one another with tears welling up in their eyes. They all knew that Lester was alone in the world and had nobody but them to turn to. If it weren't for Turkey Feather, he'd likely be homeless or dead by now.

Bill got up and turned his back to the girls. He stared out over the grounds with all his thoughts on Lester. When he was lost deep in thought, Sammie slipped up behind him and put her arm around his waist. Tina came to the other side and did the same. The three of them stood there and looked out the window together. Each of them was thinking the same thing. Even though Lester had gone to California, they were still there. What if that was them on their way to a foreign place with no friends or family. It made for serious contemplation late at night when each of them was alone to ponder the mysteries of life.

Life passed by so quickly that they had already been too busy to notice. It seemed that their lives had become intertwined, and Turkey Feather had placed its spell on each of them. They were drawn together and made complete in their humble abode tucked far, far away in the hills where the mountain laurels bloomed, and the leaves painted their vibrancy across the hillsides. Where would life take them and what adventure would they follow along the way? Would life leave them at the doorstep of another Turkey Feather somewhere in the unknown future?

As they stood there in silence, the thoughts that connected them became obvious as the passersby served to read their future to them in a surreal movie where each of them could have played the lead or all three of them could have directed the story. The strangeness of the moment seemed like a dream that had placed its grip on the unsuspecting while revealing so much truth. Finally, in the end, this would be their lot as well and it was much too painful for them to look longer and even more painful to look away for fear of having to once again face the cruel future that awaited them. Life was indeed unfair, and it was not friendly and it was forcing its will on each of them in its own miserable way.

Finally, a familiar voice awoke them all from their dream.

"What ya'll lookin at?"

Tilley had been watching Bill and the girls stare out the window. As they turned, Bill was the first to speak.

"We're just looking at the world go by, Tilley. Lots of things to see."
"Aaat's right, Bill! They sure is. What ya'll been lookin at?"

Sammie smiled at Tilley and just shrugged her shoulders. Tina walked over to Tilley and took him by the hand.

"Come over here, Tilley. Look out there for yourself. You'll see it, too."

She positioned Tilley at the center of the window and scooted his body as close to the large pane of glass as she could without pressing his nose completely against it.

"There. Now tell me what you see."

"Well, I don't see nothin' but a bunch of old people walkin' 'round. Looks like the whole lot of 'em is lost."

Tina looked out the window with him.

"Maybe so, Tilley, maybe so."

Tilley placed his arms on the window frame and peered out harder this time.

"I don't know, but aaat's gonna be you some day if you ain't careful!"

Tilley laughed but his words cut through the silence in the room like a knife. Unwittingly, he had brought the apparent to such obvious light that it shook them all awake. Bill was the first one to speak.

"I think we better get going."

Sammie and Tina shook their heads and the three of them walked to the office together without uttering a word. The previous incident had left them speechless and empty, but they knew they had a responsibility to bring Lester home.

"So, how are we gonna do this?"

"I don't know, Sammie. I guess we could all fly out there. It might be better, though, to try and track him on the train route since that's how he left."

Bill raised his eyebrows at the girls to check for approval.

"Sounds good. Bill Handley, you might just be worth a nickel after all!"

Tina chimed in, too.

"I'm not sure I can afford a trip right now."

Bill shot a glance at Sammie.

"I don't think that will be a problem, Tina. We have plenty of money to run things here, now."

"Whatcha mean? I thought we were hangin' on by a thread and a loose one at that."

"Well, like before, I'm not sure how much of the conversation you heard when we started talking about Lester going to California, but there's been a lot more going on around here than just Lester and the boys finding a cannon."

"A cannon? What in the world are you talkin' about, Bill?"

"I'll explain later."

"Thanks, Sammie. I don't think I can go through another round of all the drama that is Turkey Feather for a while."

"Drama? What drama?"

"Relax, Girlfriend...I got this, and I'll explain it all on the trip."

"Trip? What trip?"

Bill and Sammie looked at one another and burst into laughter at Tina's utter confusion. Their inside joke was going to be a blessing telling

Tina everything that had been going on. Even Sammie didn't know it all and was excited to hear the rest of the story herself.

"Okay, girls. Let's go home and meet back here in two hours. We'll go over to Queens and get our tickets and see if we can't figure out how to follow Lester McManamay on his little jaunt. Sammie, can you get a baby-sitter for a couple of days?"

"No problem. Mom will take care of it for me."

"Okay. Tina, can you get your crew set, too?"

"Roger that, Chief."

"Sounds like a plan, then. We'll meet back here and head to Queens in two hours."

The three of them gave one another a high-five. Each of them headed home to take care of the arrangements. Bill went to the bank and checked on the Turkey Feather account. Sure enough, the money was available to draw from. If this was any other place or any other time in his life, he would have thought he was caught up in something illegal with his buddy, Larry. Even though it was Lester that was first and foremost on his mind, Bill couldn't help but think of the possibilities for Turkey Feather given the access to Claudia's money. Bill felt like Santa Claus getting ready for his yearly visit to all the good little boys and girls only he was preparing to shower gifts on a lot of feeble oldsters who had held their place of dishonor on the naughty list for quite some time. Still, it was sure going to be nice to make some much needed changes at the 'Glue Factory".

Bill and the girls met up at Turkey Feather just as they had planned and they all piled into Bill's car. Luckily, the trunk was roomy enough to hold their luggage which was minimal at best. They rolled down the road feeling like distraught parents in search of their runaway child. The excitement was probably too much for them because no one seemed to have much to say. Fortunately, they were united with a singular task in mind. They were determined to get Lester back somehow, some way, and the train station was a short distance away. The only problem was how they were going to find him when they got to San Diego. It was a big place they were heading to and they weren't even sure that's where Lester was going. Trekking out on a hunch was both nerve-wracking and exhilarating in a weird sort of mix that had them all turned inside out. Finally, Bill made a nominal attempt at humor.

"Are we there yet?"

Sammie shot him a glare that could have curdled milk.

Bill looked at her wide-eyed and then turned his attention back to the road. He looked at Tina in the rear-view mirror to catch her grinning at him. He winked and she turned her head blushing. Tina was so shy that she blushed at her own shadow. Bill thought she was sweet and that she would look much nicer with a little make-up and a different hair style. She always had a friendly smile, too, just no confidence in herself. Bill felt the same about Sammie most of the time but today she was showing exceptional confidence.

In the parking lot of the terminal, they unloaded their luggage and went in. The same ticket agent was there again. He looked at their luggage and half-smiled as he turned his back to pin some papers to the bulletin board mounted on the wall behind the counter.

"Goin' somewhere?"

Bill answered with a disgusted tone.

"Yeah…somewhere. California to be exact."

The ticket agent turned around but never raised his eyes to Bill.

"Cain't git there from here. Funny, you're the second person recently to want a ticket to California. Hey…wait a minute. I remember you two. Who's the other girl? You all got a threesome goin' now?"

The ticket agent gave Bill the creeps.

"No. we're going after our friend." Sammie stepped up to the counter and looked the ticket agent in the eye.

"Look. We don't have time to fool around here. What do you mean you "cain't git there from here?" Explain what that means. This is a train station so how can you not get somewhere from here."

The ticket agent must have been brighter than he looked because he didn't try Sammie's patience any further.

"Well, Ma'am, there are different routes. This is the Cardinal route, and only goes so far. If you wanted to get to California, you'd have to plan it out and catch different trains along the line. It's not like flying. People don't take trains for the convenience. They take it for the nostalgia or because they can't afford a plane ticket. They'd buy a bus ticket, but train people are loners, and they don't want to be bothered. Sometimes honeymooners go by train."

He looked at Bill and winked over the honeymooner part.

Sammie turned and looked at Bill, then at Tina. The three of them knew that Lester couldn't have planned a trip like that in a fit of anger, so it was hard to tell where he was.

Bill stepped up to the ticket window.

"How far can someone go from here?"

The ticket agent shrugged his shoulders.

"Depends on where you want to go."

"How far could someone go if they were trying to go to California?"

"I'd say Chicago would be the farthest. Cardinal line ends there, and you'd have to catch the Southwest Chief, then the Pacific Surfliner over in Los Angeles. That's about a three-day trip. It's not an easy one, neither."

Bill pulled out a wad of cash.

"We'll take three tickets."

"Wow. Somethin must be goin on right real serious for so many people to be goin' to one place from this little old terminal. Not many people use us anymore. That beach will be crowded with the lot of you all."

"What beach?"

Bill held his breath.

"The one you're all goin', to. That's where that fella what bought that ticket the other day was goin'. Some beach out in California."

The ticket agent handed Bill the change and the tickets.

"WHY DIDN'T YOU TELL US THAT BEFORE?"

Bill yelled so loud it echoed off the walls of the terminal.

"I couldn't di-vulge in-fermation on a person to just anybody but since you all are a-goin to the same place, I can talk about it like small talk."

"For Christ's sake, do you know what could happen to that old man?"

111

Bill sounded like Sammie now.

"How was I supposed to know what he was up to, Mister?"

Bill swiped up the money and the tickets from the counter.

"How much longer before the train arrives?"

"You're in luck. It's supposed to get here in 19 minutes. Have a seat and enjoy the wait. It's time for me to go on break. I'll see ya in fifteen minutes."

Bill and Sammie picked up their bags and walked over to a bench to wait. Tina was looking at the brochure display and picked up a few to look at on the trip. When Tina came back, she sat down quietly with Bill and Sammie and looked through her brochures like an innocent child dreaming of going to faraway places. Bill imagined Tina had never had many chances to travel so this was likely a big treat for her.

Fortunately, the train arrived seven minutes early. The ticket agent wasn't back from his break. Bill and the girls followed the signs on what to do about boarding the train. An Amtrak employee met them at the door of the train and helped them put their bags in storage. The entire car was empty except for the three of them so they were able to sit where they wanted. Tina took a seat across the aisle from Bill and Sammie and looked out the window. Once they were all settled and the train started to move along, Tina became as chatty as a kid on their first big trip. She and Sammie talked about the sights along the way while Bill nodded off and slept. Through the clacking and the rushing of the wind outside, Bill would occasionally hear the girls giggle about something and then he would nod back off to sleep.

There's something about the rocking and reeling of a train car that is peaceful. Bill found it calming and Tina found it fascinating to watch life literally pass by while she looked out the window. Sammie seemed to drift off into a deep trance of sorts like the train was taking her away from a lifetime of struggle and misfortune that had befallen her at no fault of her own. Through half-open eyes, Bill watched Sammie for ever so long until he drifted off again into his own slumber of thoughts and ponderings. Bill had become more of a thinker these days what with his duties at Turkey Feather and with having to babysit the boys all the time to make sure they stayed out of trouble. Some of those thoughts fell on what to do about Turkey Feather and the facility itself but now with the money available to spruce things up, those thoughts were practically non-existent courtesy of one Claudia Saltzmann. Bill thought more and more about his own existence these days and how could he not? With all the old folks at Turkey Feather, he was practically faced with death or demise at every turn.

A thing like that can get to a person after a while and lately it had begun to affect Bill quite a bit. Maye more than he let on, but he knew it wasn't healthy to be around all that loneliness and solitude all the time. It wouldn't be long before he acted and talked like those he was taking care of and then someone would be taking care of him before he knew what had happened. Bill turned in his seat at that thought.

He tried to rest on his side, then he felt someone gently smooth a jacket over him. He raised his head a little to see Sammie standing over him.

"I'm gonna get Tina and me a sandwich from the dining car. You want somethin'?"

"Not now. I'm fine but I appreciate it."

"No problem."

Sammie gave him that crooked smile she always gave when something was on her mind. After upsetting her, he thought it was probably a better idea to let her alone with her thoughts and let her come to him if she wanted to talk. He had hoped she would talk to Tina some and let him think. It looked like he was going to be able to achieve that goal until Tina started yammering away at all the sties. She was literally like a kid on her first trip.

"Tina, are you enjoying this trip? You act like it's your first time away from home."

Tina looked at him with serious eyes and blushed.

"Well, it is my first trip. I'm sorry that I'm all excited. I ain't never been to another state before. We didn't have much growin' up and Daddy never took us anywhere cause he was too busy workin'. We all just stayed home and raised gardens and sewed and stuff."

"Oh, wow...I didn't mean anything by it, Tina..."
"It's okay, Bill. I know ya didn't. I ain't mad at ya or nothin'. I just appreciate you takin me with you and Sammie. I feel like a little kid to be honest with ya."

She grinned at Bill, and he smiled back thinking how kind-hearted Tina always was.. Bill thought the world of Tina and Sammie both but there was just something completely innocent about Tina.

113

When Sammie came back with the sandwiches, she sat down with Tina and the two of them ignored Bill for the next hour or so. It gave Bill more time to plan his strategy on finding Lester. If the ticket agent was right, there would be no way that Lester could make all the transfers on all the trains so, at some point, Bill hoped he would find Lester stranded at a train depot plotting to see what his next course of action might be.

"Hey, Bill. Whatcha gonna tell Hilda about us leavin'?"

Sammie and Tina both giggled at Bill while he looked at them with a blank stare.

"Funny, ladies. I forgot all about telling her what was up. She's probably grilled the boys to death over what all has happened and what they've been up to. I guess I better give her a call the first stop we make. Geez…I dread that call."

The girls giggled again and shrugged their shoulders indicating they were glad it wasn't them having to make the call.

Bill stood up to stretch and told the girls he was going to see a man about a dog which was code for finding the men's room. He walked down the aisle and opened the connector space between the cars. He passed through a couple of cars before he finally found what he was looking for. He was relieved to find it clean. On his way back, he grabbed a bag of peanuts and a brochure. Oddly enough, it was a flyer on the service to California. Bill's mind began to race with thoughts of Lester being lost in California again. He could kill Lester right now but would sure be glad to see him when, and if, they found him. That 'IF' was what Bill worried about most.

Bill went back to his seat across from the girls and they chatted a little about the train and its amenities and how they were enjoying the trip. Unfortunately, they did not enjoy the reason for the trip and each of them was worried to death about Lester. Why would he do such a fool thing? Getting angry was one thing but to run off like a mad man was another. He had orchestrated some pretty rotten little jokes at Turkey Feather, but this took the cake. Bill just couldn't find a justifiable reason for his behavior, and he was quite perturbed at Lester over it all. He couldn't risk scolding him when, and if, they found Lester for fear of him taking off again. Bill certainly didn't want to restrain Lester from harming himself because that would only further widen the personality chasm that had been created. Bill's hands were tied at this point, He figured he may just have to let the girls work on Lester to calm him down and reason with him.

Bill had been surprised by Lester in the past, but this stunt was totally out of character and Bill couldn't think of why Lester was acting so differently this time. He and Bill had disagreed before, but Lester had never acted like this. Bill was sure there was more to this story than what there appeared. He looked out the window and watched the fields and trees as they passed. It was sort of like watching the residents at Turkey Feather earlier that day with Sammie and Tina. Bill watched the cows and horses and occasionally a farmer out working the fields. Bill wondered what the story was as they passed each little house or building. He mused at the thoughts of the daily lives of the people who lived or worked there and thought it such a shame that their story would never be told. Again, it all pointed back to Turkey Feather because the stories there would never be told, either. Such vast knowledge that could be used by someone. So many stories of humorous events or intriguing experiences would be lost forever. Bill would never be able to write them all down even if he wanted to. Lifetimes are ever-emerging even as their story is being told. Memories give birth to new memories and sometimes even new pain. The scars don't seem to heal quite as neatly as one would like and years of ruminating on them only caused their presence to be even more noticeable. Yes, time heals all, but the memories remain to nag at us and cause us to wonder about why things happened and if something could have been done differently. Time was not kind to those at Turkey Feather. Time wasn't kind to anyone for that matter.

The train began to slow down and Tina and Sammie stretched in their seats. Bill rolled his head toward them and asked how they were doing.

"We're okay. Gotta go pottie, right now."

Tina had a good idea and Bill thought he would follow her when the train came to a full rest.

As the depot came into view, Bill stood up and looked out the window. It was almost as if they had never left, and their trip had never begun. The terminal looked so similar. The faces were the same, too. When the doors opened, Bill made his way to the exit and stepped down onto the concrete. He went in and found the facilities and took a quick but hopeful look for Lester just in case. Of course, he was nowhere in sight. The ticket agent was busily going about his work so Bill thought he would check with him to see if Lester may have come by.

"Excuse me, Sir, have you seen an elderly gentleman come in walking with a cane? He would have had a newsboy cap and maybe a trench coat that was a little raggedy looking?"

"Partner, we get all kinds of old fellas come in here lookin' like that. There's not much to do here in this town. South Shore Kentucky ain't exactly the best place in the world to come for a vacation and folks here mostly just pass through without blinkin'. Anything wrong?"

"Well, me and my colleagues are looking for him. He and I had a few words, and he left the care home we operate. It's not safe for him to be out on his own like this so we came looking for him."

"I see. I know what you mean. Father-in-law is the same way. Every time he gets mad at one of the kids, he takes off and goes for a drive somewhere. Usually comes back in a few hours. My mother-in-law gave up on chasing him down years ago, so we mostly don't pay much attention to his poutin' anymore."

"Well, that's what we usually do, too, but this time he really blew a gasket and took off. We got a lead on where he might be headed so we're going to try to catch up with him."

"Say…was he a tall fella? Sort of squinty-eyed?"

"Yes! He is tall for his age, and he does squint quite a bit."

"Well, now that you mention it, I think he may have come in here for a minute to use the restroom. That's what most everybody does here. Didn't have anything to say and just got back on the train."

Finally. That lead could help a lot.

"I sure appreciate the information. I think we might be on the right track."

"Sure thing…no pun intended with the track statement…"

"Right!"

Bill went back outside to find the girls. They were walking up and down the platform surveying anyone they could find to talk to about Lester just like he had done with the ticket agent.

"Hey! Sammie! Tina! I think I have a lead on Lester!" They came running and looked at Bill with child-like excitement.

"Yeah? What'd you find out, Boss?"

Tina could sound so innocent sometimes that Bill laughed at her anticipation.

"The ticket agent said he remembers seeing a guy that looked like the description I gave him of Lester. I think we're close to finding him. He said he got back on the train which means he probably didn't switch anything up and we may be right on his heels."

Sammie looked at Bill and asked quietly.

"Did he say anything about him getting anything to eat or drink? He's probably cold and hungry."

Bill admired Sammie for her caring nature, but Lester wasn't a lost puppy. He was a grown man with all his faculties, so Bill wasn't too worried that Lester was going to starve. He was more than resourceful for an older guy and could fend for himself.

"No, he didn't mention anything about him getting anything to eat or drink, and I don't think he would have had a chance to get it here, anyway. Lester is sharp. I'm sure he can find something to eat or drink if he gets too hungry."

"Did he say where he might be headin'?"

"No, Tina, he didn't, but by the way he got off the train and then back on, he's probably heading the same way we are. This is one of the main routes to California and he could only go so far in another direction before the line ran out and then he'd have to take another route. I'd say Lester was thinking about going straight for his target and not worrying about throwing anyone off his trail."

Sammie put her hands on her hips and looked at Bill and Tina as if to say don't mess with me right now.

"Okay, then. Let's get back on the train and see where it takes us and see if we can gather any more clues on where he is."

Tina headed to the train.

"Roger, that."

Bill grinned.

"Copy."

Sammie rolled her eyes at Bill and followed him onto the train.

When the three of them got back on the train a million thoughts ran through their heads. The idea of Lester being harmed or laying in a ditch kept coming back to them time and again. Finally, before dark, Tina and Sammie dozed off while Bill kept watch. He mulled over the time he'd spent at Turkey Feather and thought about all the things he had witnessed and the miracle of that night at the party when Claudia had sung and how she had held the entire place mystified in her gnarly little hand that had withered away so long ago. Bill thought about that day in the woods, too, and how Lester had flown off into a rage and why. That was the question he couldn't figure out. Why? Lester had always kept a cool head about him no matter what, but this was something he had let get the best of him and Bill needed to know what it was.

The night was drawing in around the train as it rocked and reeled over the rails and the rhythm of the wheels made Bill drowsy. The girls were still sleeping so Bill took the moment to catch up on some reading. He reached up and turned the courtesy light on and pulled out a magazine from under the seat. There were a few choices but the one that caught Bill's eye was one on finances and saving for the future. He thought it might be a good read and that he might pick up a few tips for retirement or how to handle Claudia's big estate. With all the excitement going on, he hadn't had one second to think about that mess. Bill chuckled to himself thinking there was no way that Hollywood could come up with a story like that if they had wanted to.

Up ahead, Bill saw the lights of a little town and the headlights of the cars passing through. Bill had always been fond of sleepy little towns, and he wanted to find one to retire to someday. The thought of staying in Nickleville had run across his mind a time or two but he didn't want to end up like the people he watched over at Turkey Feather. That thought scared Bill to death like most people who took the time to think that far ahead or to witness the slow decline of one's health and body. The loss of a mind, though, was the worst to watch. It's one thing to watch someone lose their mind to alcohol or drugs or even a disease but to lose it in a way that you don't even know you've lost the memories and the ingenuity that you once had was the most terrible of all losses. Except for maybe the loss of pride from having to start all over again in a world that was unfamiliar to you and at an age when you really weren't able, the loss of the collective experiences at Turkey Feather scared Bill out of his wits. This was ironic he thought, because when someone began the descent into the loss of their memory, they really couldn't be scared anymore. Unfortunately, there was nothing left in the end but an empty shell of what they once were which is how Bill saw it possible unfolding for himself in his mind and that was the terrifying part.

The train ride seemed to go on for an eternity, and Bill was getting restless. He couldn't sleep because of the anxiety, but he felt it was his duty to stay awake while the girls were resting. Bill made the most of the situation by trying to console himself with positive thoughts. That never seemed to work much for him, either. He thought about his childhood and how he grew up. That always brought out a lot of emotions for Bill, especially when he thought about his grandparents. His grandfather could do anything and was a very talented man. His grandmother was a musician unequaled and the two of them adored Bill with all their hearts. He was their favorite grandchild and the sun rose and sat in him. Bill was glad they drifted away on their own and didn't have to experience a place like Turkey Feather even though it was homey and caring enough. He knew he couldn't have stood to see them deteriorate.

Bill checked the map he had picked up in the lobby before they left and looked it over. He imagined all the places Lester could have jumped a train or given them the slip, but he still felt like Lester was going all the way to California as quickly as he could get there. If Bill knew anything about Lester, he knew he was more of an all-or-nothing kind of guy who set out to accomplish things in life no matter the cost or time involved. How else could he have kept up the search for that treasure all these years? When a man sets his mind to something as important as a treasure, he pretty much sets himself up for a lifetime commitment.

"Dear God…that cannon…" Bill whispered to himself in the darkness.

What would they do about the cannon? Surely, by now, one of the boys had cracked and told Hilda and the whole staff at the Smithsonian had probably descended upon Turkey Feather by now. Bill could certainly understand the fact that Lester would be upset over something like that happening. This was their trophy and their passion. They wanted it handled delicately and properly. They wanted it handled their way and their way alone. This was something they had spent a lifetime working on and they didn't want it taken from them by a bunch of scoops or ignorant meddlers who wanted to come and see an old cannon without appreciating the history behind it or the effort it took to find it. If the boys thought things would come to that, they would more than likely just want to leave it in the ground and not mention it again. Just the satisfaction of having been the ones to find it after all those years was good enough for them.

The train kept rolling for what seemed a month of Sundays and finally it made another stop. Then another. Then another. Bill lost track of where they were by now and drifted off into the night sleeping beside the girls. He was sure in his heart that Lester had decided to go on to California and there was no point in stopping much more to check on who had seen

Lester or if they had talked to him. Bill could feel it down deep that Lester was going to the end of the line like always. Finally, in Chicago, the train was coming to a stop for a four-hour layover. The crew would have to transfer to a bus for a while and then back to a train later. The whole trip was ridiculously complicated. As Bill and the girls were discussing the intricacies of the route and how hard it had been already much less what they were going to encounter with bus transfers and the rest of the trip, something occurred to Bill. With all the planning involved and the logistics one had to coordinate for a trip like this, there was a real possibility that Lester hadn't left in a fit of anger after all. There was a good chance that he had been planning this for a while and that he may have used the argument and storming off as a ruse to throw everyone off. It wasn't uncommon for Lester to take a ride on his own without the boys at times so his pouting would have normally been thought of as normal. Bill felt a sickening in his stomach like he knew he had been drawn into something. He thought he was so knowledgeable and smart about things and knew all about people. If it was a case of being fooled, then Bill and the girls were all back to square one. He dared not tell Sammie about his newfound fear because she was aggravated with him enough. That would only send her over the edge. If Bill was even remotely on to something with this new development, then he had no idea what Lester was up to now. He could only wait to see how this thing would roll out.

"Is something wrong?"

Sammie was awake and standing next to Bill's seat.

"Hmmm? Oh…no…nothing's wrong…just thinking about some things."

"Me, too. I had a dream about Lester while I was asleep. I dreamed we found him safe and sound. Hope it comes true."

Tina stepped up about that same time. She had been listening to the conversation per her custom.

"I do, too. This train is makin' my butt sore, and I'm worn out. I can't imagine what this trip would have done to Lester. He was old and worn out to begin with."

The three of them chuckled at Tina's blunt statement.

Bill smiled.

"I think we should grab a bite to eat and sort out how we're going to handle it all when we do find Les."

"Yeah, he's gonna be riled up still if he sees we been chasin' him down across the country. He likes his privacy somethin' awful."

Bill and Sammie knew Tina was right about Lester's privacy. He had always had a fierce defense of his privacy. Obviously, his pursuit of the canon and the sneaking around with the boys at Turkey Feather had been the primary reason for that. Lester wasn't much of one to share his thoughts or feelings and he played his cards close to his chest. Bill considered it a true honor to have been let in on the secret with the boys and he could see how the whole effort had become so contagious for them. A lifetime of a secret marriage to the pursuit of a treasure had taken practically everything the boys had. Fortunately, they found Bill to help them out at the last stage.

Bill and the girls made their way through the terminal and found a small hot dog joint just down the street. They read the menu and decided on a Chicago dog since they were in the area. When the order came up, they looked at one another in disbelief.

"What is that?" Bill asked.

"Well, it looks like it's a pickle on a bun with some salad fixin's on it."

Sammie shook her head.

Tina looked at it and made a funny face.

"I know I might be a country bumpkin but that ain't no hot dog like I've ever seen and I was practically raised on the things."

Bill felt the pickle on his and made a face like Tina did.

"Me, either…"

Sammie was the brave one.

"I'm tryin' it. I'm starved."

She bit into her hot dog and rolled her eyes. "You're not gonna believe this, but this thing is pretty good!"

Bill looked at her like he had looked at the hot dogs when they were brought out.

"You sure it's not because you're so hungry?"

"Could be but it's not bad. Go ahead. Try it."

Tina picked hers up and looked at Bill as if to say, "I will if you will…". They each took one in hand and silently counted to three before taking a bite.

Bill was pleasantly surprised, and Tina stood with an astounded look on her face.

"It's not as bad as I thought but it's not like the ones back home. I guess people think puttin' slaw and chili together on a hot dog is weird, too, but I this ain't too awful bad like ya said."

Tina munched on hers and mumbled something about "any port in a storm…" and Bill and Sammie grinned as they watched her eat. They all grabbed a Coke and walked around outside taking in all the sights of the Windy City. The wind was whipping up and down the streets and they certainly figured out how Chicago got its nickname. Bill picked up a newspaper and looked through the classifieds to see what the job prospects were. Even in a big city like Chicago it seemed like things were tight in the job market. A lot of specialty employment and quite a few minimum wage jobs to be had but nothing Bill was interested in. Still, it was good to see what was out there and to keep an open mind.

Tina found some ice cream and she and Sammie got a cone. Bill declined due to ice cream giving him gas. He didn't have time for any more discomfort than was necessary on this trip. Bill looked around the terminal and then up and down the alleys on the off chance that he might happen to find Lester wandering around. Of course, there was no chance of such luck and Bill gave up the search after a while. He thought more about the possibility of Lester planning this whole thing and grew somewhat angry the more he thought about that idea. If Lester had planned the whole thing there had to be a reason but, again, Bill was at a total loss for the reason at this point. Being at square one was not a good place to be on such a mission.

While Bill walked up and down a few of the streets, he tried to envision some of the notorious historical activities the town was famous for. He was a bit nervous with the girls out of his sight. He wasn't their father and he figured they were savvy enough to find their way back. He didn't want to seem condescending regarding their requests for girl time, but he was a bit ashamed of himself thinking they might get lost like two hillbillies going to town. Bill noticed a small barber shop. He knew Lester liked to be groomed well during the few occasions he and the boys would take off on their private jaunts and thought that Lester may have stepped in to get a shave or cut.

Bill walked up to the window and looked in. Black and white tiles lined the floor and there were a couple of chairs down the right-hand side of the place. The barber was ab older fellow with white hair. He was oiling the clippers while a young Asian boy sat in the chair and waited impatiently. It brought back a lot of memories for Bill. He hadn't been to a real barber shop in almost twenty-five years. The only barber that had ever cut his hair up till then had died of a busted heart and Bill was forced to stop in wherever he could find a someone to cut his hair as quickly as possible. He had mixed results with this strategy down through the years. He had even attempted to cut his own hair a time or two without much luck. The smell of the Barbicide and shave cream was familiar. Lester would have indeed stopped into a place like this on a whim.

The barber nodded his head at Bill when he walked in.

"How we doin'?"

From the sound of his accent, the barber was unmistakably from Chicago.

Bill nodded back.

"Pretty good. How 'bout you?"

"Not bad. Not bad. You're not from around here, are ya? Come in off the train?"

"Yes, sir...I sure did, and, no, I'm not from around here at all. Pretty far off to be honest."

"Sounds it. Down south way?

"No, not too far south. West Virginia. You know – over near Richmond."

Bill bit his tongue when he added the Richmond part.

"West Virginia?! Wow, you're the second fella this week that's been from West Virginia to come in here."

"Mister, you just made my day. I'm here looking for one of the folks we house at the care home I run. Me and a couple of girls from the facility are out here looking for him. If there's anything at all that you could help me with, I'd sure appreciate it. It's very important that we find him."

"He done somethin' wrong? Most folks who come through here on the train are runnin' from somethin' or someone or they're in a mess some way."

"No, no. Don't get me wrong. He's not in any trouble at all. He left in a fit and we're trying to get him back. He's older you know, and he doesn't need to be alone in unfamiliar settings."

"I remember. He did seem old and a little frazzled, but we got him cleaned up real nice here. He talked a while about goin' to California to the beach out there. He told me that him and his wife had been there, and he was goin' back to remember her. He had it all planned out and was telling us all about where he was goin'. Seemed like he was tryin' to recreate the trip he and his wife had taken a long time ago."

The boy in the chair turned to the barber.

"Look, Mister, I gotta get outta here so could you please cut my hair and let me go?!"

"You punk kids think you know everything. Shut your trap and I'll get to you as soon as I'm good and done or you can take off lookin' like a freak with your hair half cut. I'm sure Momma would love that."

The boy sunk back into the chair. He knew the barber was right about his mother.

Bill pressed.

"Did he say anything else?"

"Not much. He seemed to have a pretty good plan in place sounded like to me, though. Had the route all planned out and knew what he was doing. Sounds like he had planned it for a while."

Bill was relieved to know his hunch had been right and he and the girls were on the right track. He talked with the barber some more about what route Lester planed on using and the barber tried to recall as much as possible. Bill was putting his own plan into place now and was sure they would catch up to Lester before he could get to California.

"You don't know how valuable this information is to us. Is there any way I can repay you?"

"Tell ya what, next time you're in here, you get the full treatment, and we'll call it even."

"Thanks, Mister. I'll do that."

"Not a problem. Name is Buddy, by the way. Bud for short."

Bill tipped his forehead to Bud and walked out the door to find the girls. Bill was rushing around in a heated excitement looking for Sammie and Tina. He couldn't wait to share the news with them. He looked up and down the streets and alleyways again only this time for Sammie and Tina. Finally, he found them window shopping a couple of blocks down from where he left them.

"Hey! I think we might be on the right trail! I have good news"

"What? What is it?"

Sammie was standing with her hands on her hips again.

"I looked around and found an old barber shop. It looked like a place Lester would go in to and so I took a chance on checking with them. A guy named Bud told me a man fitting Lester's description had come in there to get cleaned up and talked about going out to California. He said he was from West Virginia, so it had to be him. From what he told me it looks like Lester may have been planning this trip for a long time, so it wasn't the argument that sent him off. He had a plan to leave all on his own."

Tina looked at Bill and hung on his every word.

"Well, I'll be...that old coot! Gettin' all of us all worked up like that! He oughta be ashamed of himself. Wait till I get a hold of him."

"We'll have to handle things delicately so we can get him back to us. If we spook him, he'll bolt again."

Bill hated to sound like they were trying to catch a wild animal but, for the most part, they were.

Sammie looked at Bill with that worried look again.

"What do we do now?"

"There's not much more we can do except for what we've already been trying. There shouldn't be but one or two more stops before we reach California. I don't think we'll need to check around anywhere else. Bud said Lester was intent on making it to California regardless of how hard the trip would be. Let's just get back on the train when it's time and ride this thing out. When we get to California, that's where the REAL search will start. Once he gets there, who knows where he could end up."

"Should we try to call home and tell them we think we might have found where he's goin'?"

Tina had a good point.

"I guess we could call and just reassure them that everything is okay. Tell them that even though we haven't found him we're on his trail. That should shut Hilda up for a while and give the boys some peace of mind."

Bill knew the boys would be worried about Lester and they deserved to know something about his whereabouts and welfare. He even suspected that they may have had some idea of Lester's big plans for his journey. No matter now, though. They had to concentrate on finding Lester as soon as possible. Planning aside, his health was no match for the toll a trip like this would have. Bill thanked his lucky stars that all the boys weren't on the lamb together. That would have surely been a disaster waiting to happen.

"Sammie, do you think you can make the call to Hilda? I'd rather not do it right now."

"Only if you insist."

"Please?"

"Oh, all right. You are REALLY going to owe me for this one!"

Tina snickered and turned her head. Something odd about her reaction to Sammie talking to him that way. Bill shrugged his shoulders and rolled his eyes then gave Tina a funny look. She put her hands behind her back and smiled like a schoolgirl that knew a playground secret.

Bill and Tina waited on Sammie to return from the phone call. When she returned, she gave Bill a look that could have withered roses.

"That bad, huh?"

"I hung up on her. She started rambling on about everything under the sun and wouldn't shut up, so I had to. I told her it was something important and I had to go."

"Well, at least they can't say we didn't try."

Sammie darted her eyes at Bill and motioned toward the station.

"Let's go to the station and grab a shower and change clothes before we get back on the train. I think that might make us all feel a little better."

Bill was impressed with Sammie's observation skills.

"Yeah, maybe we can get another hot dog or something else to eat, too."

Tina was right. It was hard to travel on an empty stomach and a shower sounded good, too.

Bill huddled with the girls.

"Let's go for it but we have to be quick. It's almost time to board the train again. I'll see if I can find us something hot since I can shower faster compared to you two."

"Sounds good. We better get going."

The three of them scrambled to the showers. When he was finished, Bill found a sandwich shop and bought a bag full of food. The three of them met back up and went to their seats on the train. Once they had settled back, silence kicked in, too. This had been a long, hard trip to this point, and they weren't even close to being finished with it. The sandwiches were good, but they all wanted a real bath and one of Hilda's hot meals. Bill thought about spilling the beans on Claudia, but he wasn't sure how they would take it. It had to be handled delicately as did all things associated with Turkey Feather. The personal affairs of the residents there were sometimes as delicate as them and Bill was sensitive to their privacy and rights. It was a matter of respect more than anything.

Tina and Sammie took to playing word games, counting cows and other things along the route to keep their minds occupied. For a while, Bill found solace in the barber shop revelation. Talking to Bud made him think of the barber shop he visited with his grandfather as a kid. All the older men sitting around telling jokes and playing pranks on one another. Man-talk always made him feel like he was more than a kid and not a popcorn fart in a windstorm like his great uncle always used to call his grandfather. Bill smiled at the thought of that old barbershop, and it helped ease his mind for the time being. Those guys had gone on to the big barber chair in the sky years ago.

CHAPTER SIX

Bill watched Sammie and Tina laugh and talk. It was time, he thought. Time for them to know the truth about Claudia and the truth about Mr. Rounder and her sister. This could be just what the three of them needed to get through this whole Lester thing.

"I have something to tell you two. It's not easy and I didn't mean to keep it from either of you. It's just something that needs to be handled right"

"Yes, Bill, we know...all things have to be handled right."

Sammie looked at Tina and they both giggled at Bill's expense.

"I mean it, Sammie. This is serious." He looked at her sternly.

"Wow. Okay. Go ahead. We're listenin'."

They both smiled at Bill so he wasn't sure they were totally into giving him a committed audience, but he was going to try to be as serious as he could to get the gravity across.

"You know how no one ever knew much about Claudia? Well, I found papers on her that had slipped down behind a filing cabinet in the office. When I opened it, I didn't know what to make of it. A lot of the paperwork was in German and some of it didn't make sense at all. There were some numbers, and I didn't know what it all meant until I found a letter from a lawyer in the back of the file. It had specific instructions for me to follow which didn't make much sense, either. I called him and got him on the phone. He was hard to understand at first and a lot of what he was saying also didn't make sense. Finally, we connected with one another, and I began to understand what he was talking about. Claudia had a very hard life. She was taken prisoner during World War II with her sister. They were tortured and Claudia was almost killed during the whole ordeal. I think she had a total breakdown. To make a long story short, she made her way to Texas and her sister and Mr. Rounder became very close. So close that they were married for a while. They divorced but remained close. Claudia's sister turned to Mr. Rounder. She asked him to take care of Claudia and he obliged. Claudia's sister was quite wealthy from the chocolatier business she ran and she and Mr. Rounder both had giant hearts.

She and Mr. Rounder made an agreement that when Claudia died, the money that was to be used for Claudia's care was to go to the facility and the facility could use it for whatever purpose needed so long as it went for the care and rehabilitation of the residents at the facility. The administrator was set to use the money as the felt right. Now, all that said, I am letting you know that that things are going to change at Turkey Feather. They're going to change a lot. A LOT."

Tina was wide-eyed.

"Are we gonna get fired?"

"No. Not that kind of change. This will be good change. I promise."

"Well, there are a lot of things that wrong with Turkey Feather and it would cost a bundle to fix all of them."

"Sammie, we're not going to have our Turkey Feather anymore. We're going to have a facility like you've never seen before."

"Huh?"

"I promise you on this one."

"How could money from Claudia help out like that?"

"Well, it's not what you think. Claudia didn't just get a regular monthly stipend. Claudia was worth nineteen million dollars. That's enough money to make sure we never have to worry about anything again."

Tina and Sammie looked at one another with their jaws hung open. They didn't know whether Bill was joking with them, and if he was using Claudia's death as a joke, it wasn't very funny to them.

"Bill, you had better not be jokin' about all of this."

"I assure you, I'm not. This is for real."

Bill was sort of giddy looking at their reactions. He could envision a completely new facility. Maybe tearing the old one down and starting over. There would be rehabilitation equipment, more activities, better food, more staff…everything. It would be a dream come true. He knew Sammie and Tina were still in shock. He hoped they would share in his enthusiasm for the new plans. Bill could literally see residents running and playing like kids. Frolicking around the grounds. He laughed out loud at seeing that sight in his mind. Sammie And Tina must have thought he was laughing at them.

"Stop laughing! Are you being serious? If you're not, we're gonna kill you. This ain't nothin' to be jokin' about. Poor old Claudia was a mess and you better not be jokin' about her."

Tina was pretty upset. Bill figured she would be excited and ask for a raise which he fully intended to give her.

"No Tina. I swear to you it's not a joke."

"Are you sure?"

Sammie had her eyes slanted like little daggers in case Bill was joking.

Bill raised his hand.

"Scout's honor."

"Oh my God. I can't believe this. Who would have ever thought Claudia was so rich?"

Tina piped up.

"Can I get a raise?"

Bill busted out laughing.

"Of course, I knew you were going to ask, and I already have it down! You too, girl."

Bill nodded and smiled at Sammie.

The three of them sat and looked at each other in silence while they dreamed of the possibilities. The wheels were turning so fast they almost forgot about Lester and had to re-focus. It would mean so much for the residents. They all knew that. They were all thinking the same thing. It was just too good to be true but, this time, it really was true. This would mean so much for everyone, including the staff. Sammie and Tina knew what it would mean for them financially and Bill could certainly use a vacation. Claudia literally held the power and the future of Turkey Feather in her gnarled, little, dead hand. The reality would set in when they told the residents and Hilda. Dear God, Hilda.

Bill already felt like Santa Claus but now it was time to tell them about the cannon. He didn't think they would be nearly as excited about the cannon as they were about the money, but he figured he would let them in on the secret.

"I have more. There's also a certain something about Turkey Feather you should know about."

Tina shifted in her seat.

"Uh oh. Here comes the bad news."

"Not bad news. Just more news. It's not even news. It's more like a secret to be told. A secret that is intriguing and unusual. I've already told Sammie most of this but there wasn't time to think through all the details to tell you or the others. You see, all those times the boys at Turkey Feather were off on their little trips for the day, they weren't exactly visiting sick kids or having picnics. They were really treasure hunting."

"Treasure huntin'?!" Tina exclaimed.

"Yep. Treasure hunting. Turkey Feather was a special place during the Civil War times. There was a lot of activity going on and a certain Captain by the name of Fink seems to have stolen and buried a cannon and maybe some gold. He was a soldier gone rogue and built Turkey Feather with means that no one could really figure out how. He even wrote a poem of some kind that tells where the loot is hidden. It's kind of convoluted. To make a long story short, the boys have been looking for this rumored cannon and anything else the Captain may have hidden for nearly a lifetime. That's what drew them all together. They've been friends for decades and have been on this exploration for years. It all sounds strange but, apparently, they were possessed by the thoughts of finding the treasure to the point that it drove them away from their families and everything else. It literally took them over and stripped them of their lives. The funny thing is, they've kept this secret up for all these years until I came along and got suspicious and started poking my nose into it. They hated me for it at first, but when they knew I had the goods on them, they came clean."

"Sounds like they were committin' a crime. I can't believe those guys. They seem so innocent."

Sammie almost teared up.

"They are."

Bill interjected.

"It's not that they're criminals so much Sammie, it's just that they lost their lives to something that was a dream and they let it take over everything."

Bill watched Sammie as she turned away and looked out the window. He knew she was thinking of something that she, too, had been pursuing all her life. Sammie only wanted to be accepted and to be treated with love and respect. He didn't know how to provide that to her without taking their relationship farther than what he thought she might be able to take on right now. He didn't know if that was something he had even thought about enough to start to think about. Their relationship was confusing and while he had started to ask her out once or twice, he didn't know how that would go over at Turkey Feather. Hilda would certainly make something out of it and there were the residents who might have thought it was cute and quaint, or who may not have cared one bit. Tina was in the picture as well. She was a bit flirtatious sometimes and gave Bill a smile more than a few times. Bill liked Tina. She was a little free with her laughs and letting her hands brush over his back. Bill liked both girls and tried not to differentiate between them. He could sense that there were possibilities between the two of them. Possibilities that could ruin some things but maybe enhance others. Bill would have to think on that more when he was off the wild Lester chase.

"That's sad that they let that happen but maybe that's what their passion was. Maybe that was what they wanted to do and didn't mean to hurt anyone. It's a possibility that they didn't mean for ay of it to happen and that they just got caught up into something they couldn't control. Something that took over."

Tina sounded pitiful and looked as if she was going to cry. Bill and Sammie sat for a minute until Sammie finally took her hand.

"Are you okay?"

"I'm fine. I just know how life can be sometimes and how it can suck everything out of you even after you give everything you've got. It crushes you."

"It's okay, Tina. I know life is rough. Looks like things might be gettin' better soon."

Tina smiled.

"Shore hope so!"

She and Sammie laughed and hugged.

Bill sat there not really knowing what to say. He let the moment pass to the girls.

"Now, we've got to get back to finding Lester. If my calculations are right, he should be well on his way to California and has about a day's head start on us. Since we're pretty sure we're on the same track as Lester, I think it's best that we just keep on following him like we have been. We might even get lucky and find him along the way if he decided to take a break. If he didn't, and I don't think he has taken a break because it looks like he had his own agenda, then we're just going to have to find him when we get to Ocean Beach. That friends and neighbors will be like looking for the proverbial needle in a haystack. If we're lucky enough to find him, we can only hope he's okay and in one piece. If there's anything wrong with Lester, we'll have to get him to a hospital and have him tuned up before we take him back."

"What if Lester doesn't want to go back? What if he wants to move out here somewhere and live out his time in California? What do we do then?"
Tina looked afraid.

"Good point. Lester is fully capable of making his own decisions and we would have to honor his wishes if he decided that. That would be hard, but we would have to let him be at that point."

Bill was proud of himself and felt like a general before going out onto the battlefield. He looked at Sammie and Tina. They acknowledged the plan as it was. No more questions. They were going with it as is. Once they reached Los Angeles, they would take the short trip to Ocean Beach and start looking.

Two more days passed, and the ride seemed to go on forever. Same old scenery, same old cows, and the same old rusty railyards just like the song says. Bill was bored out of his mind by now and felt like Willie Nelson at this point riding on the City of New Orleans. Bill imagined in his thoughts the lives of the people they passed. He dreamed up stories of farms and factories and all the little intricacies of life that made up the rail line view. He fancied himself an amateur writer and thought he could spin a yarn or two from all that he saw. Interesting stuff to be written about for sure.

Bill nudged Sammie to wake her. They had already seen the California welcome sign a day earlier. Up ahead the Los Angeles sign was in sight. Tina started to wrest herself from the grips of sleep about the same time. Their excitement was growing. They knew they had a long row to hoe ahead of them and they only hoped they were ready for the challenge. Exhausted and still hungry, the small meals and sandwiches they had eaten along the trip was growing on their patience. The first order was to get showers and wash out their clothes in a sink somewhere then get a good meal to get them going. Everything was falling into place and the plan seemed to be unfolding as the train pulled into the station.

Bill stepped off the first and headed to the first terminal he came to. Tina and Sammie took their belongings and followed behind.

"Excuse me, but could you tell me where we could get a shower? We've been traveling from West Virginia and we're looking for a friend of ours."

The lady behind the ticket booth pointed and said, "Head straight out that door and follow the signs. YMCA and YWCA both are down the street."

"Thank you very much."

Bill and the girls picked up their bags and headed toward the door when the lady behind the counter stopped them.

"Did you say that you were from West Virginia? Looking for a friend?"

Bill turned to the lady and replied.

"Yes, we are. Why do you ask?"

The lady behind the booth pointed again.

"You lookin' for him?"

Bill and the girls turned their heads simultaneously in the direction she was pointing.

"I'll be…"

Their mouths all dropped collectively and made a popping sound.

There, at the other end of the terminal, sitting at the end of the row of chairs was Lester McManamay in all his glory. The three of them hadn't seen a sight for sore eyes like that in a long while.

Bill looked at the woman.

"How in the world?"

"I know, seems like a miracle. Where did he come from? He's been sitting here in the terminal for almost two days. He's not been any trouble. Got plenty of money. Been coming and going like he owns the place. He's had coffee, pastries, goes out and comes back in. Talks to people like he's known them all his life. We just thought he was a strange old fella from wherever. People drop in here all the time in a lot worse shape than him, but he seems to have it all together."

Bill tried to explain.

"Well, he started off as a refugee from a care home, but we think he's been planning this trip for a while. He and his wife spent some time out here when they first got married and it's kind of a long story after that."

"Yeah, that's what he told us. He's been treating everyone like family around here. He' a cool cat. Fits right in around here."

Bill was astounded.

"What has he been doing?"

"Like I said, he fits right in. Even brought me a coffee. When you said you were looking for a friend from West Virginia, I kind of put two and two together."

"You don't know how much you've helped us."

"No problem. Take care of my little friend."

'We will."

Bill turned to the girls.

"Can you believe that?"

Sammie and Tina stood silent and shook their head in disbelief.

"Me, either. I guess this is show time. Better let me go to him first so we all don't spook him by rushing up at once."

Sammie and Tina stood silent and shook their heads in agreement.

Bill walked up to Lester as gingerly and as possible. About ten feet away, Lester turned and looked at Bill.

"I've been wonderin' if you were nosey enough to follow me or not. How'd you figure out where I went."

"It wasn't easy, but it wasn't that hard, either. I remember some of the conversations we had, and I looked through some of your belongings.'"

"I figured you would go snoopin' through everything."

"Not snooping. Just looking for clues. Clues that we needed to have to find you. We were all worried. Sammie was sick over you and Tina has had to calm her down the whole trip."

"You dragged them along with you? I bet you went and ran your mouth about the treasure and everything, didn't you?"

"The conversation did come up. I had to tell them why I thought you left so it would make sense. Then I also thought maybe you had left for other reasons."

"Other reasons? What in the Sam Hill reasons would I have to leave? I ain't got no place to go and nobody to go to. I just wanted to get away from you and the rest of that bunch. I'm sick of people and I just want to be alone."

"Alone? The woman at the booth over there said you had been walking around here like you own the place and talking to everyone like you were old friends with all of them."

"Brenda? She keeps comin' over and checkin' on me like I'm some little kid. Bugs the daylights out of me."

"She seemed fond of you when I talked to her. She told us that you fit right in around here."

"Aaahh...what does she know? She just meddles in people's business like everybody else."

"I see. So why DID you come all the way out here to California? Taking a trip down Memory Lane? Maybe going back to where it all started?"

Lester scowled.

"What do you mean, Memory Lane? What are you gettin' at?"

"I think you came all the way out here to relive some of the memories you had with your wife. I can't figure what else would have possessed you to take the trip all alone."

"I TOLD YOU! I want to be ALONE."

"Lester MacManamay, you are one of the nosiest and most sociable people I know. You want to know everything that goes on EVERYWHERE all the time. You can't fool me. I know something is up."

"Aaahh…you wouldn't understand it anyway. I don't want to talk about it."

"Lester, you can either talk to me or one of the girls because not one of us is going to leave you alone until you spill the beans about this whole mess. I know you're not still mad. That's not your nature. Something triggered the trip and you and I both know it."

Lester looked off into the distance. A tear began to roll down his cheek.

"You don't understand, Bill. I'm done. I don't have anything left but a few old pieces of the past that I can't hold on to. Time won't let me."

"What do you mean time won't let you hold on to anything?"

"I'm dying."

Bill gave a long pause before he responded. "How long have you known?"

"Ohh… few weeks or so. Not real long."

"Why didn't you tell us?"

"I didn't want pity. Besides, I've done about everything I wanted to do, and no one is left for me to turn to. I just wanted to die alone out here where I had been happy once. Where Millicent and I had come on our Honeymoon. We were young and full of dreams back then. The whole world was our pearl. Nothin' could stop us. We were gonna have it all."

Lester fell silent and lowered his head in thought. He continued the story looking at the floor.

"I found good work while we were out here but there was something that nagged me about home. I knew we should have stayed but we didn't. Millicent was a small-town girl and couldn't leave her mother alone. She begged for us to go back. I loved her so much that I would have followed her anywhere she wanted to be. There was never any question about that. When we got back home, the only work was the mines, of course, and I didn't care for that kind of stuff. I wanted to be something. Somebody. I wanted to make a name for us. We hadn't planned on having kids so that wasn't much of a worry. I got my certificate and started teaching school. It gave us the summers off to travel and start something that we could be proud of and turn into an enterprise."

"We were like two peas in a pod. We did everything together. We were inseparable. Then, life threw us a curveball and she started having spells. At least that's what we called them. She saw every doctor we could find and afford. Nobody could tell us what was happening to her. Millicent would lose her balance and her hearing, and she would be bedfast for days at a time. She tried to maintain as best she could, but the spells eventually disabled her. Toward the end, she was having them all the time. She suffered day and night and all I could do was watch her. Finally, she died on me, and my heart was broken."

Bill placed his hand on Lester's shoulder.

"I'm sorry, Lester."

"Don't pity me. I don't want that."

"When did you meet the boys?"

Lester chuckled sadly.

"It took a while for us to all cross paths. I loved history and got wind of the cannon story decades ago. I researched everything I could find and rifled through a lot of the same stuff you brought in. One by one, we connected. We had history clubs back then and our social media was going to the diner and drinking coffee. Eventually, we put the Quartet like you call it together and we got a plan up to start looking for that blasted cannon. Newspapers and reporters came out to poke around into what we were doing or make fun of us or whatever they were doing but it put our names in the paper. Basically, gave us all inflated egos. We had the fever. We had been bitten by the treasure bug. We became married to it and each other in some sort of strange journey that we couldn't explain. It took us over. We didn't care. We liked the attention and the thought of finding a treasure was too much to give up. We left everything we had behind. Day and night we worked on that thing, researching, and hiking around in the woods looking for something that would bring us closer to what we were looking for. We didn't even know what it was that we were looking for. We couldn't see the forest for the trees, you could say. I guess I'm to blame for it all. I was the leader because I had so much time on my hands. The others were just as dedicated as me but there was something that I couldn't let go of. I can't explain it. I'm ashamed of it for the most part because I know all the trouble it caused the boys with their families. I felt like a cult leader. I liked the taste of power it all brought me.

We finally zeroed in on Turkey Feather from some old documents we found in a barn that was on the original property. A lot of the property had been sold off for developments and the farm itself had changed quite a bit. About all that was left of the original estate was the little bit of property around what we call Turkey Feather now. Back when the cannon disappeared, it was called the Fink Estate. Even though we were looking for that old cannon, there was the possibility of other treasure, too. I guess maybe that's what really drew us. Like I said. We had no idea what we were really looking for so the possibilities of wealth beyond our wildest imagination became real to us. All we wanted was a little piece of the pie like everybody else."

"I can understand all of that, Les. I really can. You found it, though, so why leave now?"

"You don't get it at all. You just can't understand, Bill."

"What is there to understand? You spent a lifetime looking for something and you found it. A million people look for something their entire lives and never find anything. I guess I really don't understand why you're so upset over this whole thing or even what you would be upset over."

"That's just it! IT'S OVER NOW!" My life…it's over…there's nothin' else left to look forward to. I don't have anybody to share it with. Nobody that cares about me or what's important to me. Those old coots all secretly resent me for what I stole from them as their "Fearless Leader". They blame me for losing all they had, too. I didn't force them to do it. They caught the fever themselves. I didn't do anything to them. They're probably dreamin' up a plot to kill me now. I didn't do anything to 'em. I tried to lead 'em. Now it's all gone from all of us. Once we were strong. Now, we're just a bunch of old busted up relics that are no good to anyone. All I wanted was to go to the beach that Millicent and I went to on our honeymoon for her sake. It was going to be my way of showing her how sorry I was about letting her down with my life and how that I had meant to take her back and how I made a mistake and took her away from her family. I never should have brought her out here and tried to make her leave behind everything she loved.

I came out here and got scared and hoped that someone would come lookin' for me because I just can't go on. I'm scared and I hurt. The sickness is makin' me weaker. I can feel it. I failed Millicent and myself. I failed the boys back home and I've failed my whole life. I just wanted a chance to make some things right. I couldn't even make it to the beach if I wanted to, now."

Tears began to roll down Lester's cheeks. He turned away from Bill and looked down the length of the station. Bill didn't quite know what to say except for a few words of encouragement.

"It's okay, Lester. It's okay."

Bill reached out his hand to Lester's shoulder. When he touched him, Lester bowed his head and began to cry openly. Bill looked behind him and motioned with his head for the girls to come over and be with them.

Sammie and Tina shouted out his name and began running toward Lester.

"Don't let them see ya cry, les. It'll only upset 'em."

Lester wiped away his tears as quickly as he could and stood up to face the girls. He mustered a smile and opened his arms for the girls to hug him.

Sammie was first.

"Don't you EVER do that to us again, Lester Macmanamay! You could have been hurt, or killed, or anything!"

"Not much worse than gettin' killed could happen, I suppose!" Lester retorted.

"Shame on you! We love you!" Tina scolded and hugged him and cried all in the same breath.

"I promise. I don't think I could make another trip like this one if I wanted to. I'm sorry I led you all on a wild goose chase. I guess it was more like an old coot chase runnin' after me, though."

"Why did you do that?"

Sammie looked up to him like a child looks up to their grandfather.

"I had my reasons, young lady. Long time has passed since I felt this alive and loved. I had to come out here and try to remember again."

Tina blinked.

"Remember what?"

"What it's like to be young again, and alive one more time."

Sammie and Tina began to cry. They hugged Lester even tighter.

"Lester, why don't we all get cleaned up and go grab us a meal. I know you're bound to be hungry. A hot shower would make you feel better."

"Thanks, Bill. I think I'd like that."

Lester looked at Bill with a genuine but tired gratitude. They both understood one another. Bill felt as though they were closer than ever now. The girls left Lester's grip and walked out of the station in search of the YWCA. Bill helped Lester with his belongings. They walked arm-in-arm to the YMCA. Bill was surprised at how much weaker Lester seemed. He was either tired or he was being affected more by the sickness than he realized.

When everyone was 'all gussied up', they found an old-fashioned breakfast restaurant where they could all find something they liked. Lester was famished and ate everything he ordered and drank as much water and coffee as he could hold. He talked about a lot of things at that breakfast dinner but never mentioned the illness. It wasn't time for the girls to hear about that. He and Bill had forged an unspoken agreement to keep that a secret. The conversation went back and forth about Turkey Feather and how Lester's trip went compared to their own until everyone had talked themselves out. Bill took that opportunity to make a gesture toward Lester and his condition.

"Lester, I have a proposition for you. Why don't we get a couple of hotel rooms this evening and relax? Then, first thing in the morning, we can all go over to Ocean Beach and spend some time there. You could walk around and make your peace with the past and we could just hang out and wait for you. Would you like that?"

Lester looked as solemn as a statue.

"I think I'd like that a lot."

Everyone smiled at their new plan. The girls put their heads down to allow Lester and Bill to have their father-son moment without interruption. Out of the corner of his eye, Lester let a tear drop slip down his cheek and then caught it with a flutter of his eyelids.

The gang finished up and left a nice tip for the waitress. They found the closest hotel and Lester and Bill paired off and went to one room while the girls took the other one.

"Hey, Bill – can we raid the liquor cabinet?"

Tina laughed and Sammie snickered at the suggestion.

"Hey, why not? We've got plenty of money!"

They gave each other a wide-eyed, open-mouthed look of surprise and giggled like two schoolgirls practically breaking down their room door. Lester gave Bill a funny look at the mention of plenty of money and Bill reassured him.

"No, we didn't sell the cannon. I swear."

Lester dropped his eyes and chuckled.

"Come on, let's get settled inside." Bill held the door for Lester and helped him with his bags. Lester was packed lightly but the trip had been hard on everyone, including Bill.

When they got into the room, Bill flipped the access card key on a table and told Lester he could have his pick of the beds.

"I think I'll just take this one right here…"

Lester patted the bed and sat down on the edge.

"I'm going to go check on the girls and see what they're in to."

"Don't do anything I wouldn't do!"

"I'm too tired to do anything at all right now!"

The two of them chuckled and Bill left the room. Lester sat on the edge of the bed and pondered his good fortune to have found Bill and Turkey Feather.

BIll knocked on the girls' room, but no one answered. Then from behind the door, more giggling.

"Who isss it...?"

"It's me, silly. Open sesame, or else."

"Oh, Sir...we don't talk to strangers. They might be bad men. We're sweet and innocent little girls and we're afraid of big bad men."

"Oh, brother. You two would get sent back with an apology note attached if anyone kidnapped YOU!"

Uncontrollable giggling from behind the door now.

"Goodbye. Let me know if you need anything."

"We will, you big bad man!"

More giggling.

Bill shook his head and walked back to his room. Who knew what troubles the two of them would find before morning? Bill laughed to himself and opened the door to his and Lester's room. As he walked in, he saw Lester lying down. Quietly, he walked over and stood by his side. Lester wasn't breathing. Bill was mortified at what he saw. He gently nudged him, but there was no stirring. Bill hung his head and sat down beside him. He cried when he realized Lester was farther along than he had let on in the station. Maybe he didn't know how advanced the illness was, but Lester was gone from them for good.

Bill didn't know what to do. He hated to tell the girls what had happened because they were having such a great time and they would likely not get a chance to do this again for a while. Bill waited until an answer came to him that sounded fair to everyone. He would wait until the morning to tell Sammie and Tina and sit up with Lester. It would be another one of the stories that Lester and the boys used to laugh about. They sat up with the dead when they were younger which was the custom. Bill poured himself a drink from his own mini-bar and toasted Lester, and the cannon, and the quartet. It was going to be a long night. Bill poured another one. He watched over Lester throughout the night and reminisced about their journey together. Lester was put in Bill's life for a reason. He hoped he understood and figured he had learned a valuable lesson over wasting one's life but, somehow, he got more out of it than that. Perseverance, determination, and commitment...all the things in life that help you achieve your goals. He didn't know what would become of the knowledge he had amassed from Lester except that he knew he would need to write it all down and remember as many details as possible. Bill felt a sickening in his stomach. He had lost his best friend. Nothing at Turkey Feather would ever be the same after this.

CHAPTER SEVEN

When morning came, Bill waited to screw his courage to the sticking point. He called the local authorities and requested that someone come to the room to fetch Lester's body. He hated to talk to Sammie and Tina, but they had to know. Bill knocked on their door. There was no answer. It was still early so they may not have been stirring yet. Finally, he could hear someone moving around in the room. Tina opened the door and looked at Bill with an inquisitive face.

"Hey Bill, what's up? Are ya okay? You look like you haven't slept all night. You and Lester have a wild party?"

"No, nothing like that."

Bill went silent. Tina took his silence on cue.

"Here, come on in."

Bill walked in softly.

"Uh...where's Sammie?"

"She's right in here. I'll go get her."

"Hey, Bill. What's up? Everything okay?"

"Well, no. It's Lester. I found him this morning. I came in last night after checking on you two and he was lying on his side still in his clothes. He must have passed in his sleep."

"NO!" Sammie yelled.

Tina sank back into a chair.

"I knew this was too good to be true."

Bill felt a twinge of guilt, but Sammie didn't say anything to him. She just sat on the couch and buried her head in her lap and sobbed. Tina looked out the window.

"What do we do now?"

"I've already called the authorities. They're on their way. I'll explain the situation to them. They'll make the arrangements to have his body sent back home for us."

"Are you okay, Sammie?"

"I'm fine. I knew this would happen. I had a dream about Lester last night leavin' again. I had a funny feeling this morning that somethin' was gonna happen. I'm just glad we got to him and let him know how we felt about him. I knew that somethin' would happen."

"Sammie, I'm sorry. I didn't' mean to…"

"Bill, it's not your fault. I know Lester took off on his own and he had a plan to sneak out on us. I know it wasn't you. I'm just upset and I'm sure gonna miss him. He was like another father to me."

"I know he was, Sammie."

For the second time in as many days, Bill had no idea what to say.

The authorities finally arrived and took care of Lester with Bill. The questions were all answered, Lester was covered over with the white sheet, and the arrangements were made to have his body shipped back to West Virginia. That was it. In thirty minutes, a lifetime had been summed up with the actions of a few emergency personnel and no one would much think of Lester McManamay again. Seemed so unfair but Lester had pretty much passed from society when he came to Turkey Feather. It was, after all, its own death sentence and Lester had lived it long enough. His body was wheeled outside where Sammie and Tina stood vigil waiting for him to pass. Sammie hung her head to her chest and reached out to touch the sheet as he went by.

"Could I have a lock of his hair before he moves along?"

The Emergency Medical Technician looked at Sammie hesitantly. He reached into his pocket and pulled out a long pair of scissors and snipped a few strands of Lester's hair. He handed them to Sammie before he covered Lester back over.

"Thank you."

Tina hugged Sammie from the side and Lester began his final journey back home. That was the end of the Turkey Feather Quartet.

Tina and Sammie went back to their room and gathered their belongings. Bill made the call to Hilda and swore her to secrecy about Lester. He felt it was his personal duty to let the boys know their "Fearless Leader" was gone. They would appreciate the information more from him. As the three of them were leaving the hotel, a notion came to Bill.

"Hey, you two, we're not on any time limit now so I was kind of thinking that maybe we could do something before we left if you don't mind."

Sammie looked at him with the saddest of eyes.

"What did you have in mind? I'm not in much of a mood to have fun or go out."

"Me, either. I was just thinking that maybe we could go over to Ocean Beach and visit for a while in honor of Lester and Millicent. Maybe we could say a few words and watch the ocean for a while. Sort of like a make-shift funeral of sorts."

Sammie smiled amidst her tears.

"That sounds fine to me."

"Okay, let's find a bus that will take us there. I think the terminal is down the street. It shouldn't be a long trip."

They found a bus terminal and boarded their ride to the beach. It was only a few minutes to the beach, but they traveled silently the whole way which made it seem to last for hours. Everyone was completely exhausted at this point and losing Lester was the final straw. None of them could take anymore.

Bill grabbed his bags and stood as the bus came to a stop.

"Here we are."

Sammie and Tina got their bags, too, and swung them in front of their legs to make it easier to move. They were so tired, they looked like toddlers trying to keep up with an adult.

When they stepped off the bus, they could smell the beach air. It was unmistakable. Sammie and Tina had never seen the ocean and Bill had never seen the Pacific. They looked around for a bit completely silent. No one really wanted to be there, but they had to do it for Lester. They knew that. The way they all felt they could have been going to their own funeral.

They made their way to the beach area and scooped out a place that looked suitable for their purpose. As much as they tried to not think about Lester, they also tried to let his spirit guide them to a spot on the beach he would have approved of. They walked down to the pier and found a place in the shade to have their ceremony.

"I guess this is as good a place as any for something like this."

"I think so."

Sammie sat down and waved to Bill.

"Go ahead, Preacher Handley. Do us the honors."

Tina and Bill laughed. It was nice to break the gloominess of the moment and Bill appreciated knowing that Sammie was still on his side.

"Okay. I guess I can come up with something. Let's see…How do I start? Ladies and Gentlemen, we are gathered here…"

Sammie stopped him.

"No, no, that's how a wedding starts. Say, 'Dearly Beloved…' and go from there."

"Right. Let me try again, Sister Sammie."

"Dearly Beloved, we are gathered here to honor our friend, Lester McManamay. He has parted from us and gone to the great beyond to be with his beloved Millicent. He tried to meet her spirit in this hallowed place that he considered sacred to himself and her from so many years ago. It is our sincere wish that you would rejoin them, Lord, in that happy place where they will dwell forever and ever with you and the many others they loved throughout their lives. Amen."

Bill was proud of himself. Apparently, he still remembered some things from those sermons of long ago. He and the girls bowed their heads in silence and prayed individually for Lester and Millicent. Bill was on a roll, so he continued.

"Lord, we hope that our lives will be filled with loved ones and longevity like Lester's. We hope to be able to share your glory with those others and enjoy our journey down here on Earth with the same enthusiasm and excitement that Lester showed us in example. Blessed be your name and blessed be the signs that show us you have received our prayers in earnest. Thank you in the name of Jesus. Amen."

"Not bad, Preacher Handley. Not bad."

Sammie winked at Bill and patted the sand for him to join her.

Tina stood up and walked toward the pier.

"I know that was hard for you but hopefully it will be some small token of release for us all. I think Lester would have appreciated you sayin' such nice words on his behalf. I just can't believe he's gone. All this time we've been lookin' for him, I thought we would take him home and things would get back to normal. Well, except with everything about Claudia. That still floors me."

"I know what you mean. I feel so empty right now."

"Hey guys, look at this!"

Tina was pointing at the pier.

"Do you see what I see?"

Bill stood up and walked over to Tina.

"What is it?"

"Look."

Bill looked at the pier where Tina was pointing. On a small area of an abutment about five feet up was something scratched into the concrete.

Tina turned to Bill.

"It says 'LM and MM' with a heart around it. You don't think that could be Lester and Millicent, do you?"

Cold chills went up and down Bill's back.

"I can't say for sure, Tina, but it sure looks like that's our sign that Lester made it and our prayers were heard. Can't much argue with that."

The three of them gathered and stared at the initials as the breeze carried their memories of Lester and the Turkey Feather Quartet off into the sea.

David Ricer laid down his pen and turned off the tape recorder.

"That's a pretty good story, Mr. Handley. Very touching. What happened when you all came back here to Turkey Feather?"

Bill laughed.

"We got old ourselves and now we stay here like they did!"

Sammie and Tina smiled, and Bill looked at the young man with a certain glee to tease him by withholding the information.

"I mean, how did you tell everyone about Lester and Claudia and all?"

Ricer was eager to hear more and was sitting on the edge of his seat with his mouth hanging open.

"It's sort of complicated. We got back here as soon as we could and laid poor Lester to rest. The boys were all tore up and they were never the same, really. Nothing was the same after Lester passed. The boys died one by one. After Lester went to his reward, they pretty much gave up the ghost. They all went peacefully in their sleep. I guess they had come to accept that their life's passion and goal had been achieved and, in some small way, they felt like they had contributed something of themselves to society. Something that could serve as their mark on the world. They were happy with their fifteen minutes of fame, and they relaxed on to the big glue factory in the sky. It was all a big joke and loads of fun to them and when their ride was over, it was over. No amount of medicine or machine could keep them here.

We finally got a crew in here to help us with all the proceedings with the cannon. It was listed on the historical registry and there was a big ceremony with all the dignitaries for miles around coming to see it. You'd have thought it was a real-life Civil War hero come to life. I guess, in a way, it was. People 'ooh'ed' and 'aah'ed' over it for about three or four years. It was a big thing. So many people had looked for it for so long. Nobody could believe that four old men could have researched it like they had and then just stumbled on it by chance out in the woods. A lot of people were jealous and called it a fake. We had to have some of the folks at the Smithsonian come out and certify that it was real and that it was as old as it was. That shut the naysayers down. Little kids would have their picture made with it and we even got a letter from the "PRESIDENT OF THE UNITED STATES OF AMERICA"!

Bill always added a southern drawl and a big laugh for effect when he mentioned the President's letter.

"It was quite a spectacle. Then, everybody got used to it and sort of lost interest."

Tina's hands and arms had taken to shaking some these days. Her mind was sharp as a razor, though. She was too feeble to talk about the story of Turkey Feather too long at a time, but she liked it when she had a chance to interject tidbits of interest from time to time.

Sammie had suffered a stroke, but could still write something of a scrawl a few words at a time to communicate. David looked at what she had written.

"We was prou."

"I imagine you were proud, Ms. Miller. That was a big deal for the whole community."

Bill chimed back in.

"That's a good point. We were practically a tourist trap. The news stations came out and covered the cannon story and one of the big channels on television interviewed the boys. They were thrilled with all the attention from the fruits of their labor. They were offered a hundred thousand dollars for that old cannon. Ironically, after all that searching, they decided to donate it and send it to Washington, which you knew, of course."

"Yes, I've seen it at the Smithsonian several times. It's still one of the more popular items in the Civil War exhibit. People from all over the world come to see it now."

"That's good. I'm glad they enjoy it like we did. Tilley was a little distressed when the boys let it go but he was just upset over losing the attention he got giving people the historical facts and asking everyone to answer Civil War trivia. He switched his sports trivia to Civil War after the cannon gained popularity. Tilley died a few years later. He went off his medication again and ran out into traffic in the middle of the night and got hit by a semi-truck. About the same time is when the rest of the Quartet started peeling off, too. Fred was next after Lester. He had lasted longer than anyone thought he would. Mavis was after him with a heart attack. Then there was Raymond. That rascal had been telling the truth all those years about being related to Oliver Hardy and having money stashed away. One day we got a letter here from a bank out west stating they had been looking for Raymond for quite some time. They wired the money and he upped out of there and found him a pretty, young thing just like his father. Last thing we heard about him was he passed in his sleep a couple of years later with that young girl by his side.

Funny how it all turned out. Now it's just the girls and me. I guess we're the Turkey Feather Trio."

"That's too bad about Tilley. He sounded like a character. Sad, too, about the rest of the boys. I assume their families were aware of the cannon find and came by to see them?"

"No. Sadly enough, you're wrong about that Mr. Ricer. Not one of the boys had any family members come see then after the cannon was turned into the Turkey Feather Tourist Trap – that's what they called it. It had become a burden to them all. Especially Fred. He was tired anyway and all the people always coming to see the cannon just got on his nerves. His daughter wrote him a letter and blasted him for letting the cannon come between him and the family for so long and it broke his heart. He thought they had mended that fence, but it appears that she got jealous over the attention he gave everyone else and cut him out of her life completely.

It sounds like a nice story but it's a sad one. Even though the boys found what they were looking for, they lost everything in the pursuit of their dream. That's the realization of it all. If there was some way that they could have tempered their passion and shared more of themselves with the ones that loved them, they wouldn't have died with broken hearts. In the end, it was a strange mix of the peace they found combined with the regret they carried. It was sad for us to watch them all go like they did. One by one, the residents at Turkey Feather that I started with all faded away. Hilda had even been a resident here for a while and so was Lucy. We will too, soon."

Bill looked at Sammie and placed his hand over hers..

David could see he was dealing with a touchy subject and had to choose his words carefully.

"I see...so...ummm...Mr. Hand-ley...what I really came here for was to ask you about what happened to Turkey Feather after the cannon. It seems like the facility just exploded in growth after the cannon was put on display. I hate to ask this and I hate to sound like I'm questioning the story, but there seems to be something that doesn't add up. I know the Turkey Feather Quartet story about them finding the cannon was important to the place but what happened after thy passed away, too? I mean, what happened after the donation, and you still haven't told me about how you handled Claudia's money?"

"Haha...you're very persistent, aren't you Mr. Ricer?"

"As a sworn agent of the United States Treasury and the Internal Revenue Service, I have to be."

Ricer added his own version of a southern drawl when he mentioned the treasury and internal revenue part of his explanation for his dogged determination.

"Fair enough, I guess. I hope you can understand what Claudia's money meant to us. It allowed us to invest the money into equipment and resources that brought us to the pinnacle of what this place was meant to be which was a rehabilitation facility. When Rounder was here, it limped along like a rag doll. No one had the means to keep it going much longer. It was on its last leg when I got here. It didn't make two biscuits in a bowl of red-eye gravy who was running the place, it was doomed! Claudia's money, as you refer to it, was a lifeline for us. The residents got exactly what they needed, and we turned it into a private facility so we could decide who came and stayed based on their personalities and the overall environment at the time. We even set up a board that made all the financial decisions. We were also very frugal.

People helped us in all kinds of ways. Ways that your books could never show. People didn't take pity on us. They knew that we could and would use any help we could get so we took to working deals with people for work and other things. The cannon put us on the map. Why the Devil do you think we changed the name to the Brass Cannon Therapy Estate? That blasted cannon that had taken away the lives of four good men was what gave life to dozens and dozens of others after the boys were long gone. As far as your audit, you'd have to go back twenty years before you could even begin to see that all the work that we did here wasn't done with money. It was done out of the kindness of people's hearts. We'd come in and have loads of people helping out on the grounds or working on the electricity or doing whatever it was that was needed. You can't imagine the feeling when you can just sit back and focus on the needs of the people that you're supposed to take care of.

You say you want to know about all the money was set aside for the indigent folks that we interviewed to come here. That account has grown on its own and the supplies we get are mostly donated. We're the envy of the entire elderly care industry. Were known all over the country for being experts at getting things donated to us. The only thing we're guilty of is caring for people so much that the feds want to come in and break up the party. Explain to me why that is, Mr. Ricer?"

David Ricer was certainly flustered at this point.

"Oh, no. We're not trying to cause you any distress we just find it unusual that you've flown under the radar for us so long..."

Sammie smacked her hand on the table.

Bill looked the young man in the eye and leaned toward him.

"Unusual, you say? Well, Mr. Ricer I find it unusual that you would waste your time and our taxpayer dollars to come all the way down here from Washington on a wild goose chase to bully three old farts, and badger us about how we've ran a care facility for the last thirty years without help from your 'gumment' pals in the big Ivory Tower up there in D.C. We might be from West Virginia but we're not a bunch of ignorant hillbillies."

This time there was no drawl to Bill's voice. He had grown tired of the kid from the IRS asking questions and enough was enough at this point.

"I see that I've upset you, Mr. Handley."

Tina piped up with her opinion.

"You really are a smart one, ain't ya, sonny?"

"I'm sorry. My apologies to you all. This whole situation is highly unusual and very unlikely that you have operated for so long without bringing attention from our auditing division. The good news is that you are quite correct. We've looked at your finances and your operations and there's nothing that says anything has been done that is illegal. If you will excuse me, I'll leave you be and consider this matter closed. Again, I apologize for any inconveniences or distress I may have caused you, Ms. Miller, and Ms. Dennison. While this has been our first meeting, I hope you'll forgive me for the circumstances that brought us together. It was my pleasure."

"I don't think it's been much pleasure for us."

Tina smiled at the young man as if to purposefully confuse him with the intent of her statement. Sammie waved 'Goodbye' to him in a comical gesture.

Mr. Ricer stood and reached for the door of the office.

"Thank you for your time."

As Mr. Ricer drove out of sight, the Turkey Feather Trio stood aglow as they watched him leave the grounds of the Estate. The Brass Cannon Therapy Estate seemed to be clear.

Sammie nudged Bill.

"Do you think he bought it?"

"I don't think we'll see him much more after this, if any. Sort of makes me think of how ol' Rounder high-tailed it out of here all those years ago. I believe the IRS is not as interested in Brass Cannon as they thought they were. You two were perfect, by the way. I almost busted out laughing when you smacked the table and scrawled 'we was prou', Sammie."

"What? I was just tryin' to help."

"Help? You were trying to intimidate that poor kid and you know it. I have to say you gave a commanding performance yourself. Good strategy."

"A body does what a body has to do. You know how it is."

"I do, indeed."

Bill and the girls laughed at their folly and how they had scared the 'gumment' spook away from the Estate. There had been a lot of other people come out to ask about how they had made Brass Cannon so famous. They had only ever talked to Bill, though, so he had never witnessed the true acting abilities that Sammie and Tina possessed. He was very proud of his girls. They were sure to share many laughs in the future about their ruse with the IRS man.

"Bill, are you ever gonna tell anyone what really happened with the cannon and Claudia's money?"

Sammie had her arms crossed and was tapping her foot at him waiting on an answer.

"Why should I? We've all three kept it a secret all these years. Besides, it wasn't her money or the cannon that did it. The cannon made us famous, but those gold bars were really what put us ahead. It took some doing to get those things turned into cash. I had to call every black market contact I ever had to exchange them. We even lost a few doing that. I'm surprised more people than Ricer haven't come snooping into things. We've worked hard to manage our finances and keep this place going 'under the radar' like Ricer says and I don't think we owe anyone an explanation much less the IRS. They've taken so much already, surely, they wouldn't miss a few million dollars."

"Four to be exact.:

"Thank you, Tina. Four to be exact. What we did was provide a safe and secure residence for people who worked all their lives and got screwed over by life. They lost everything because they got sick, or someone took their life savings, or they got behind on paying for a life they wanted to have and just couldn't get any help from anyone. They ran their business into the ground by trying to play by the rules and the rules sank them. We just helped them leave this world with some dignity and pride and a little peace and happiness."

"Don't you think someone else will figure it out at some point?"

"Maybe. But the 'treasure' is gone now. Nobody is going to be able to find it because we got it all. Go ahead. Look out that window and tell me if you see any of those bushes out there on the front lawn. No, you do not. You remember how happy we were when we realized the flowers on that tapestry that good ol' Captain Fink sewed for us were really markers that matched the pattern of the bushes scattered all over the place out there on the front lawn all willy nilly? You remember how happy we were when we dug up that first bush and found those jars of gold coins under it? Not to mention when we found the gold bars, too. We didn't give a flyin' hootie tootie about the Knights of the Golden Circle or subverting what may have been an important piece of Civil War history or how we got what we got. We didn't care one bit when we realized how important those coins and gold bars were and what their value was and how they could have possibly served to change the tide of American history and bankrolled the South to victory. How many years did that tapestry cost us? How long did it take us to figure that blasted poem out? We paid our dues, I think. The way I see it, we're doing a far better service for these people by paying for their needs directly than any amount of money the government could provide them would do. Besides, if they had really been that interested in all those gold coins and bars, they would have dedicated some of that money they've wasted the last couple of centuries to finding it. I think we found it fair and square and it's going to good use."

"I guess you're right, you old coot!"

Sammie hugged Bill around the waist as if to calm him down.

"Oh, I see how you're gonna be. You know that trick only works ever so often. You still try to use it all the time. Shameful."

"I think it's sweet."

Tina put her hand over her heart and patted it.

"You do the same thing. You all think you have me wrapped around your little finger and that I'll do whatever you want if you give ol' Bill a hug or a peck on the cheek. Sheesh…you'd think you'd learn better by now.

"Well, it usually works every time."

They all laughed and stared down the road far beyond the grounds of the Estate. Many years ago, they stood in the same spot and looked at the same scenery. Time had flown by and the adventures they shared were priceless. The Quartet, Claudia, the cannon, and the treasure. All of it had brought them together like a big family. Seeing as how Bill had never married and Sammie and Tina had both lost their husbands not too soon after things took off at Brass Cannon, they had become more like a family than most families. They had shared the concerns of what those before had worried about and how that now they were in the same position.

Each was keenly aware of their lot in life and not sure as to what to do about it which is exactly what kept them tied to the Brass Cannon Therapy Estate. Long gone was the Turkey Feather Rehabilitation and Assisted Life Care Center and all that they had known when they were young. The only difference is that they wouldn't be dropped off at the Brass Cannon. They were permanent residents already. The had lived on the grounds together so long they couldn't imagine what life would be like without one another. They would never know if they had missed out on the extravagances of life, but they had taken a few vacations together and Sammie's kids served as their Estate children. They came by but not as often as the three of them would have liked. The cycle had repeated itself and the Trio had watched it unfold right before their eyes. They had even helped orchestrate it which gave them something of a degree of satisfaction.

There were certain things they couldn't control, though, which gave them moments for pause. The ruse with Mr. Ricer was fun for the time but it wasn't too far off from the truth. Bill was slowing down. Sammie found it harder to get out of bed in the mornings. Fortunately for Tina, she seemed to be as happy go lucky as always and took life one step at a time. They had done well for themselves some would say, but the Trio placed all their satisfaction on the fact that they felt like they had done well for others. Altruistic as it may have sounded, they really meant that in their hearts and thought it had been a noble thing they had done. There certainly were needs being met and no one had suffered financially for it. Everything was done above board so who cares if it was cash or where the cash came from. They had settled this moral argument amongst themselves long ago and Bill was determined to stand by their decision. The girls always got nervous when people started to poke in their business. Bill had learned to ignore it for the most part. He had lost very little sleep over it but not enough to make him change his mind.

Bill broke the silence.

"You two finished worrying about things again?"

The girls laughed at his fatherly tone.

"Yes, Pa, we're finished."

Sammie smacked Bill on the butt.

"I mean it's not like we're criminals, you know. We're more like Robin Hood and his Merry Men only it's two merry women. Nobody has ever been harmed. I like to look at it like a big pot from a private poker game."

Tina spoke up for Bill.

"'aat's right!"

The three of them burst out laughing when Tina imitated Tilley. It had been a long time since he had livened things up at the Estate, so it was a perfect opportunity to finally loosen up.

Tina and Sammie went about their regular routine. The had brunch together and retreated to their rooms. The three of them had lived a good life of leisure since that cannon and tapestry had changed everything for them. Bill was proud to have helped make things easier on them. He had enjoyed things that he liked, too, especially the fishing trips and hunting trips he had taken over the years and the leisure time to write a few books under his nom de plume, Lester Tilley. Sammie loved her children very much. She understood they were busy and had to live their lives the way they saw fit, and she was determined not to interfere the way her father had done in her life. Sammie was content.

Tina genuinely enjoyed life and was so thankful that Bill and Sammie had adopted her. She had often thought of Bill and Sammie as her parents even though she was a few years older than them. She realized that her lack of education had put her in a unique position all to her own, but things hadn't turned out too bad for her. She picked on both Sammie and Bill and told them often it was time for them to get married. Bill blushed when she made mention of marriage, but Sammie seemed intrigued about the idea. She still flirted with Bill as did Tina but there was a certain spark between Bill and Sammie. Down deep, Bill knew this and so did Sammie. The situation with the Estate had always kept them from pursuing anything serious.

Bill heard a knock on his office door.

Thinking it was Sammie, he answered in that familiar tone from years ago.

"Who iss it?"

"It's me, Tina."

Surprised, Bill rose from his desk and answered the door.

"What's up?"

"It's time."

"Time for what?"

"You know what. The 'what' I've been tellin' you for years. You two have been at this long enough. I saw it today as plain as day and you need to do somethin' about it. That girl has been waitin' on you to ask her to marry you for umpteen years now. Get off your duff and do it. We're not getting' any younger and it's breakin' my heart to see my two best friends in the whole world that are closer to me than my own family ever was stay separated like this. Now, Bill Handley, you better do somethin' about this or I'm spillin' the beans on everything!"

"What?! Tina!!! You wouldn't! We'd all be shamed! We didn't even do anything illegal!"

"I don't care. I've lived this life long enough of secrets and hidden feelings between you and Sammie and I wanna see some action."

"You do, do you?"

"Yes, I do. Now get to it."

Tina left the office and went about her routine.

Bill was surprised at Tina's blunt attack, but he figured if anyone knew the situation, no one did better than her. He sat back down and thought it over. Bill had always been a thinker way more than a doer. This time he knew he was up against a wall with Tina. Over the years, she hadn't stated her piece but a few times and when she did, she was right on the money.

Bill screwed his courage to the sticking point once again.

"I'm going to do it."

He picked up the phone and dialed the conference number three-way for Sammie and Tina.

"Could I see you two in my office, please?"

"Oh my. Please. This must really be good."

"Come to the office and you'll find out, Miss Sammie Miller."

In a few minutes, the girls were knocking at the door. He opened it without answering their knock which was a rarity for Bill.

They came in and sat in their favorite chairs.

"Better make this good, Chief. My show is on."

"Sammie Miller, will you marry me?"

Sammie stared blankly at Bill. "Do wha…?"

"You heard me. I did not stutter. I've loved you since the day I laid eyes on you. I even bought this after our first Christmas party together when Claudia wowed us all."

Bill pulled out a one-carat diamond engagement ring from his pocket and opened it. Even Tina gasped at that turn of events.

Pointing to Tina, Bill began his explanation.

"Thanks to your friend here, I've been threatened with nothing short of murder if I don't do this. We've practically been married for years but I want to make it official. Will you be my wife?"

Tears began to fall from Sammie's eyes. She sobbed uncontrollably.

"I never thought you'd ask. I always hoped you would, but I never thought you would do it. Why did you take so long? I felt like I wasn't good enough all this time or smart enough."

"It wasn't that at all. We've been together so long, I never thought I would have to ask. I guess I just figured it would magically happen somehow or that if we did things would change for the worse and we 'd lose all we had worked for."

"You mean like what happened to the boys. Yes. I know I's late in the game, but I don't want us to live our lives like they did and just wake up one day and be dead. I want us to make a life for ourselves now. God knows we've almost wasted a lifetime like they did. We need to move now and make the best of what time we have left."

Tina was crying in the corner and honking her nose like a foghorn.

"Bill Handley, you old coot. You've given me a lifetime of memories already and I'd be proud to have you as my husband."

"Tina, come on."

"Huh? What do you need me for?"

"A witness."

"Oh. Okay."

"I need you as my Maid of Honor, too. You're all I have left."

Tina was honored and was so proud of her friends. Even though she knew things would pretty much stay the same, she had done some good for her friends and her as well.

Sammie and Tina hugged and the three of them ran to the parking lot as fast as their now aging legs would carry them. Bill had a newer Mustang now, but it was still the same color as the old one. They hopped in the car, let the top down and backed out of the driveway. They watched as they passed the facility and recollected all they had done and the lives they had touched. They remarked to themselves how their lives had become so intertwined. Each touching the other in so many ways. All of them were happy as they drove down the long, snaking driveway from the Estate.

It was past the first part of autumn and a lot of the trees had already begun to change. The colors dotted the countryside as they drove along the highway. The air had a crispness to it that brought a smile to their faces. Off they went into the autumn of life.

ABOUT THE AUTHOR

P. RAY LEWIS is a former high school science teacher and regional representative for the United States Senate in the office of U.S. Senator John D. "Jay" Rockefeller IV. He holds advanced degrees in both Secondary Education and Teaching.

Mr. Lewis currently resides in Beckley, West Virginia, and works as the Director of Career Services at Concord University. In his spare time, Phil also speaks to young adults on leadership and life choices while advising them on career pathways. Most all the writing he shares with his audience draws from real-life experiences during his time as a social worker, teacher, small business owner, Senate aid, and general observer of life.

Individuals who follow Phil's simple Facebook posts are affectionately referred to as '*Phil Watchers*'.

Phil is available to speak at leadership and life coaching conferences or events by emailing him at: p.yaylewis71@gmail.com

www.ingramcontent.com/pod-product-compliance
Lightning Source LLC
Chambersburg PA
CBHW060647260626
47161CB00008B/3030